美國
餐飲實用英語

PRACTICAL ENGLISH FOR
U.S. RESTAURANTS

Publisher: Times Publishing（NY）Ltd.
時代出版社（紐約）出版

目錄 Contents

I. 基礎篇 Basic Expressions — 5

- 6 基礎英語知識 Basic English Knowledge
- 16 餐飲一般流程及用語 Generic Process and Expressions
- 21 點菜 Taking Orders
- 23 推薦 Recommendations
- 34 埋單結帳 Paying the Bills

II. 外賣餐館 Take out Restaurants — 39

- 40 接單常用短語 Common Phrases While Taking Orders
- 46 電話接單常用句子 Common Sentences for Taking Orders on the Phone
- 51 指示方向的常用語 Common Phrases in Directions
- 58 外賣餐館情景對話 Situational Dialogues at Take-out Restaurants
- 58 外賣接單 Take Out Orders
- 63 送餐寫地址實況會話 Delivery Conversations
- 66 櫃枱接單會話 Taking Orders at the Counter

III. 堂吃酒樓用語 Dine-in Restaurants Expressions — 71

- 72 中式菜肴 Chinese Dishes
- 78 餐桌服務式餐館情景對話 Situational Conversations at Table Service Restaurants
- 78 預定座位 Making Reservations
- 85 請賓客入座 Seating the Guests
- 86 爲賓客點菜 Taking Orders
- 88 菜式介紹 Dishes Introductions
- 93 名酒介紹 Wine Introductions
- 96 用餐服務 Meals Service
- 98 徵求意見 Asking for Suggestions
- 100 用餐結賬 Paying the Bills

IV. 自助餐用語 Expressions for Buffet — 104

- 105 常用句型 Common Expressions/Sentences
- 108 會話關鍵句子 Key Expressions for Serving Guests
- 112 埋單結帳常用句子 Key Expressions while Paying the Bills

English 英 Chinese 中 Cantonese 粵

V. 酒吧服務 Bar Service 114

- 115 酒吧服務要點 Bar Service Key Points
- 115 常用句型表達 Useful Expressions
- 118 情景對話 Situational Dialogues
- 129 準備婚宴 Preparing a Wedding Banquet

VI. 宴會 Banquet 121

- 122 宴會預訂 Banquet Reservations
- 126 爲公司宴會做準備 Preparing a Company Banquet
- 132 準備生日宴會 Preparing a Birthday Banquet

VII. 日本餐 Japanese Foods 135

- 136 日本料理烹調原則 Cooking Guidelines for Japanese Cuisine
- 136 日本料理三大類別 Specialty of Japanese Cuisine
- 137 日本料理的烹調特色 Types of Japanese Cuisine
- 137 日本料理常見的菜單 Common Dishes
- 139 醬料 Sauce
- 140 沙律 Salad
- 141 面類 Noodles
- 142 天婦羅 Tempura
- 142 生魚片 Sashimi (Raw Fish)
- 144 燒烤類 Broiled Dishes
- 145 湯 Soups
- 145 壽司卷 Sushi Rolls
- 147 菜單講解 Dishes Explanation
- 148 其它菜單 Other Dishes
- 149 飯類 Donburi Rice
- 150 常用句子 Useful Sentences
- 150 套餐 Set Courses

VIII. 處理抱怨 Handling Complaints 155

- 156 處理抱怨的常用句型 Key Expressions in Handling Complaints.
- 162 情景對話 Situational Conversations
- 167 衛生檢查 Sanitary Inspection
- 171 店鋪維修 Restaurant Repairs

IX. 餐館常用詞 Useful Words for Restaurants 177

X. 附錄 Appendix 198

本書編排與使用

1. 點擊本書封面上的有聲標志 ，開啟本書有聲內容。

   點擊內文頁右上角的語言鍵 ，選擇您需要的語言。

   （注：如不選擇，您將無法聽取正文語音。）

2. 點擊使用說明頁上的音量調節鍵 ，可以調節音量大小；

   點擊MP3播放鍵上的各個按鈕 ，開啟相對應按鈕的功能。

3. 本書分為九大主題，內容全面具體，句子精煉實用。本書是在美從事餐飲業者的好幫手。他不僅僅可供您平日學習、查閱，還可以在您工作時隨身攜帶，隨時查找您想要表達的句子。書本所有內容不僅配有MP3光碟，還有好學寶點讀筆幫您解決發音問題，點到哪讀到哪，即學即用。

注：粵語部分語音不與文字對照，祗按口語習慣錄音。

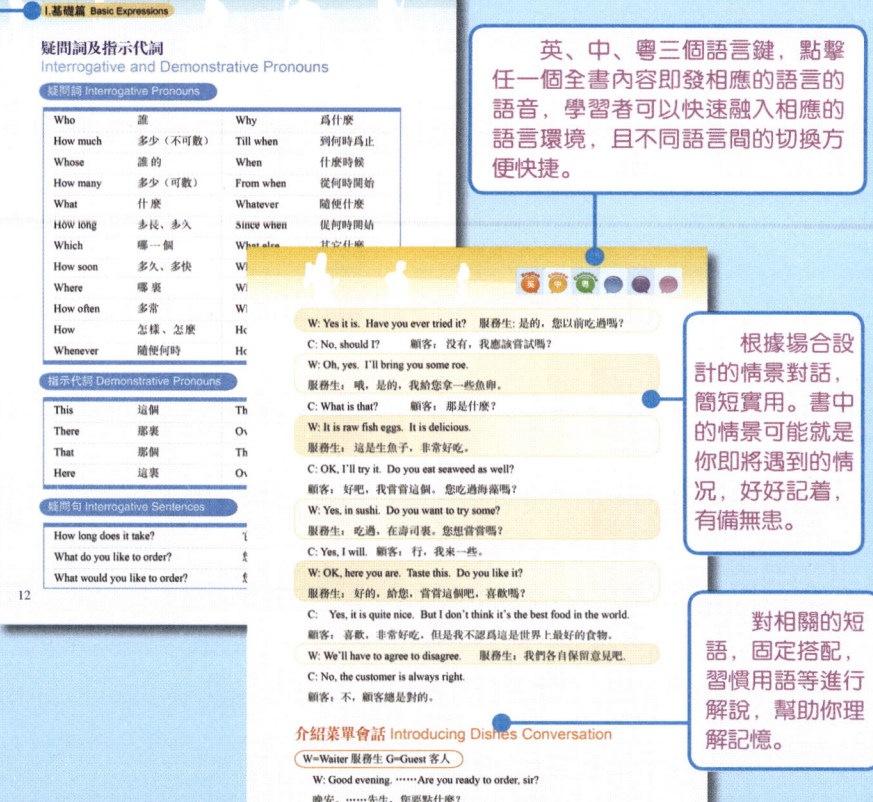

每個小主題都設計有不同顏色的索引，方便讀者查閱。

英、中、粵三個語言鍵，點擊任一個全書內容即發相應的語言的語音，學習者可以快速融入相應的語言環境，且不同語言間的切換方便快捷。

根據場合設計的情景對話，簡短實用。書中的情景可能就是你即將遇到的情況，好好記着，有備無患。

對相關的短語、固定搭配、習慣用語等進行解說，幫助你理解記憶。

與中文對應的英文表達，編者精心挑選常用表達，讓你說一口地道的口語。一些句子有多種表達方式，編者也在旁邊增加了這些相同的表達，豐富你的句型，積累多樣性的句子。

I. 基礎篇
Basic Expressions

- ✓ 基礎英語知識 Basic English Knowledge
- ✓ 餐飲一般流程及用語 Generic Process and Expressions
- ✓ 點菜 Taking Orders
- ✓ 推薦 Recommendations
- ✓ 埋單結帳 Paying the Bills

基礎英語知識
Basic English Knowledge

英文字母 Alphtabets

大寫	A B C D E F G H I J K L M N O P Q R S T U V W X Y Z
小寫	a b c d e f g h i j k l m n o p q r s t u v w x y z

美國KK音標 IPA

元音	長元音	[i]	[ar]	[o]	[u]	[ɝ]		
	短元音	[ɪ]	[ʌ/a]	[ɔ]	[ʊ]	[ə/ɚ]	[ɛ]	[æ]
	雙元音	[aɪ]	[e]	[ɔɪ]	[ɪr]	[ɛr]	[ʊr]	[o]	[aʊ]
輔音	輕輔音	[p]	[t]	[k]	[f]	[s]	[θ]	[ʃ]	[tʃ]
	濁輔音	[b]	[d]	[g]	[v]	[z]	[ð]	[ʒ]	[dʒ]
	鼻音	[m]	[n]	[ŋ]					
	似拼音	[h]	[r]	[l]					
	半元音	[w]	[j]						

數量表達 Numeric Expressions

One	一	Twenty-three	二十三
Two	二	Twenty-third	23rd
Three	三	Twenty-four	二十四
Four	四	Twenty-fourth	24th
Five	五	Thirty	三十
Six	六	Thirty-one	三十一
Seven	七	Forty	四十
Eight	八	Fifty	五十
Nine	九	Sixty	六十
Ten	十	Seventy	七十
Eleven	十一	Eighty	八十
Twelve	十二	Ninety	九十
Thirteen	十三	Hundred	一百
Fourteen	十四	One Hundred and Sixty	一百六十
Fifteen	十五	One Thousand	一千
Sixteen	十六	Eighteen-Hundred	一千八百
Seventeen	十七	Ten Thousand	一萬
Eighteen	十八	One Hundred Thousand	十萬
Nineteen	十九	Million	百萬
Twenty	二十	Ten Million	千萬
Twenty-one	二十一	One Hundred Million	一億
Twenty-first	21st	Billion	十億
Twenty-two	二十二	Percentage	百分比
Twenty-second	22nd	Eighty Percent	百分之八十

I. 基礎篇 Basic Expressions

電話號碼表達 Phone Numbers Expressions

212-123- 4560（直讀法）

Two one two, one two three, four five six O

987- 654 - 3210 （3210讀成三十二，十）

Nine Eight Seven, Six Five Four, Thirty-two, Ten

626- 987- 6533 (33，讀成兩個三)

Six Two Six, Nine Eight Seven, Six Five double Three

718-555-9700 (555-9700，讀成三個五，九十七個百)

Seven One Eight, Triple Five, Ninety-seven Hundred

金錢的表達 Monetary Expressions

金錢的種類 Types of Monetary

Moncy	金錢的總稱	Money Order	匯票
Cash	現金	Check	支票
Coin	硬幣	Traveler's Check	旅行支票
Dollar Bill	紙幣	Bank Certified Check	銀行本票
Single Bill	一元的紙幣	Food Stamp	糧食券
Dollar	美元	WIC Check	嬰兒奶票
Buck	美元（爲俗語）	Change	零錢, 換零錢
Quarter	二角五分硬幣	Credit card	信用卡
Dime	一角硬幣	Master Card	萬事達信用卡
Nickel	五分硬幣	Visa	維士卡
Penny	一分硬幣	American Express	美國運通卡
Cent	美分		

常用金钱表达 Frequent Used Money Expressions

25¢ ($0.25)	Twenty-five cents; A quarter
$8.20	Eight dollars and twenty cents
$36.25	Thirty-six twenty-five
$60.30	Sixty dollars and thirty cents
$987.65	Nine Hundred eighty seven, sixty five
$16,000	Sixteen thousand
$3,800,000	Three Million and Eighty hundred thousand
$400,000,000	Four hundred million dollars

時間的表達 Time Expressions

基本词汇 Basic words

o'clock	點鐘（如：现在七點鐘）
Hour	小時（如：七個小時）
Quarter	刻（一刻爲十五分鐘）
Minute	分鐘
Second	秒
A.M（或a.m）	上午（表示中午以前的時間）
P.M（或p.m）	下午（表示中午以後的時間）

时间常用表达 Common Expressions for Time

Six thirty a.m.	6:30 am 上午六點半
Ten P.M.	10:00 pm 晚上十點
Eight forty-five	8:45 八點四十五分

9

I.基礎篇 Basic Expressions

Seven o'clock	7:00 七點鐘
One hour	一小時
Half an hour	半小時
Ten minutes	十分鐘
Five seconds	五秒鐘
Ten to eleven	10:50 （還差十分鐘到十一點）
Quarter to nine	8:45 （還差一刻到九點）
Ten before Five	4:50 （還有十分鐘到五點）
Quarter after Seven	7:15 （七點後的十五分鐘）
Nine past mid-night	0:09 (凌晨後九分鐘)
What time is it?	幾點了？
It's six forty.	六點四十分(6:40)
Do you have the time?	幾點了？
It's quarter after ten now.	現在是十點十五分 (10:15)
What time do you have?	幾點了？
It's five before nine.	八點五十五分(8:55)

日期 Date

Year	年	Monday	星期一
Month	月	Tuesday	星期二
Day	日、天	Wednesday	星期三
Last year	去年	Thursday	星期四
Next month	下個月	Friday	星期五
Morning	早晨	Saturday	星期六
Noon	中午	Sunday	星期日

Afternoon	下午	January	一月
Evening	傍晚	February	二月
Night	晚上	March	三月
Late Night	夜深	April	四月
Mid-night	凌晨	May	五月
Today	今天	June	六月
Tomorrow	明天	July	七月
The day after tomorrow	後天	August	八月
The day before yesterday	前天	September	九月
Yesterday	昨天	October	十月
Week	星期、周	November	十一月
Weekend	周末	December	十二月

常用問句 Common Sentences

What day is today?	今天是星期幾？
Today is Sunday.	今天是星期天。
What is today's date?	今天是幾號？
Today is April 1st 2010.	今天2010年4月1日。
What is the date after tomorrow?	後天是幾號？
It is April 3rd.	後天是4月3日。

疑問詞及指示代詞
Interrogative and Demonstrative Pronouns

疑問詞 Interrogative Pronouns

Who	誰	Why	爲什麼
How much	多少（不可數）	Till when	到何時爲止
Whose	誰的	When	什麼時候
How many	多少（可數）	From when	從何時開始
What	什麼	Whatever	隨便什麼
How long	多長、多久	Since when	從何時開始
Which	哪一個	What else	其它什麼
How soon	多久、多快	Which one	哪一個
Where	哪裏	What size	什麼尺碼
How often	多常	Why not	爲什麼不
How	怎樣、怎麼	How come	爲什麼
Whenever	隨便何時	How about	怎麼樣

指示代詞 Demonstrative Pronouns

This	這個	These	這些
There	那裏	Over here	這邊
That	那個	Those	那些
Here	這裏	Over there	那邊

疑問句 Interrogative Sentences

How long does it take?	它將要花多長時間？
What do you like to order?	您喜歡點些什麼？
What would you like to order?	您喜歡點些什麼？

When should we start serving dishes?	我們什麼時候開始上菜？	
When will you be here?	您何時來這裏？	
Where is China King Buffet?	中國王自助餐在哪裏？	
Where is the restroom?	廁所在哪裏？	
Which one do you like?	您喜歡哪一個？	
Who's coming with you?	請問你和誰一起來？	
Why don't you order today's special?	你爲什麼不點一個今天的特別推薦菜？	

禮貌用語 Courtesy

常用問候語 Common Greetings

Hi!	嗨！	Nothing much.
Hello!	哈嘍！	沒什麼特別，老樣子。
Good morning!	早上好！	Pretty good, thanks, how are you?
Good afternoon!	下午好！	很好，謝謝，你好嗎？
Good evening!	晚安！	Very well, thank you.
How are you doing?	過得怎樣？	很好，謝謝你。
How are you?	你好嗎？	What is up?
How have you been lately?	近來好嗎？	近況如何？
How's it going?	近況如何？	What's going on? 你在忙什麼？
How's everything?	一切都好嗎？	
I'm fine, thanks.	很好，謝謝你。	
I'm doing fine.	我過得很好。	
I'm Ok..	我很好。	
Just as usual.	沒什麼特別，老樣子。	

I. 基礎篇 Basic Expressions

表示稱贊 Compliments

Beautiful	美麗的、漂亮的	OK	好的
Correct	正確的	Perfect	真棒
Excellent	極好的	That's great.	太好了。
Nice	爽快	Wonderful	驚奇的，好極了

抱歉用語 Apologies and Responses

Excuse Me.	對不起、打擾一下。
I'm sorry.	對不起。
Sorry about that.	對那件事、我很抱歉。
That's all right.	沒關系。
No problem.	沒問題。
It doesn't matter.	沒關系。
It's nothing.	這沒什麼。
I beg your pardon, sir.	請您原諒。
It's my fault.	這是我的錯。
Excuse me for interrupting.	抱歉，打擾一下。
I'm sorry. A guest is waiting for me. 抱歉，有個客人正在等我過去。（終止談話時用）	
I'm sorry. I'm being called. 不好意思，有人叫我。（終止談話時用）	

感激用語 Gratitude & Response

I appreciate it.	我很感激。
It's my pleasure.	這是我的榮幸。
Thank you very much.	非常感謝你。

Thank you.	謝謝你。
Thanks a lot.	很感謝。
Thanks.	謝謝。
With pleasure.	別客氣。
You're welcome.	別客氣。
My pleasure.	
不用謝！樂意爲您服務。	
Please feel free to contact us anytime.	
請隨時與我們聯系。	

告別用語 Saying Goodbye

Bye.	再見。
Good bye.	再見。
See you later.	以後見。
Have a nice day.	祝你一天快樂。
Have a good one.	祝你愉快。
You too.	你也是。
Same to you.	你也一樣。
Take it easy.	慢慢來。
Take care.	多保重。
Thank you for coming.	謝謝您的光臨。
We all look forward to serving you again. 真誠期待再次爲您服務。	
Hope you enjoy staying with us.	希望您在這兒過得愉快。

I. 基礎篇 Basic Expressions

餐飲一般流程及用語
Generic Process and Expressions

迎接客人 Meeting Guests

問候語 Greetings

It's nice to see you again.	很高興再見到你。
How have you been lately?	近來好嗎？
Glad to see you again.	很高興再次見到你。
Thank you for coming back.	謝謝你再次光臨。
Hi! Long time no see.	嗨！好久不見了。
It's been a long time since I last saw you.	從上次起，好久不見了。
Welcome to Rose Garden Restaurant.	歡迎光臨玫瑰園餐館。

迎客入座 Welcoming Guests

How many of you, sir?	你們有幾位，先生？
How many people are there in your party?	你們的聚會有多少人？
How many people do you have this time?	這次你們多少人？
A table for six, please.	六個人（一張桌六個座位的）。
Four of us together.	我們一起4個人。
Is your party all here now?	你們都到齋了嗎？
Are you expecting anyone?	請問還有客人要來嗎？
May I ask if anyone is joining you?	請問還有沒有人要來？
Is anyone joining you later?	等會兒還有人參加嗎？

詢問是否有預約 Asking Whether Made a Reservation

Do you have a reservation? 你有預約嗎?

You made your reservation in what name?
請問您是用什麼名字預訂的?

Did you make a reservation? 你預訂了嗎?

Did you reserve a table? 你預訂座位了嗎?

I have a reservation for 8 persons at 7:00PM. 我們預定了7點的八人桌。

We reserved a table for six persons at 6:30PM under the name Mr. Johnson.
我們以約翰遜的名義預訂了下午六點半的6位桌。

客人詢問有沒有桌子 Inquiring Table Availability

Is there a table for six available?	有沒有六個位的桌子?
ABC	ABC
This table is already reserved.	這桌子已經被預訂了。
Is this seat taken?	這座位有人坐嗎?
All our tables are booked up.	我們所有的桌子都訂滿了。
There isn't any table available now.	現在沒有空桌子了。

座位選擇 Seating Preference

Here's your table.	這就是你的桌子。
Your table is ready sir.	你的桌子已經準備好了,先生。
Will this table be all right?	這張桌子可以嗎?
Would you like to sit near the window?	靠窗邊的座位怎麼樣?
Where would you like to sit?	你喜歡坐在哪裏?
You can sit anywhere you like.	你可以隨便坐那裏。
Where would you prefer to sit?	你喜歡坐在哪裏?

17

I. 基礎篇 Basic Expressions

Would you like a smoking or a non-smoking area?

您喜歡吸烟區還是非吸烟區？

I think this table is too close to the doorway.

我想這個位置太靠近門口了。

Would you please bring one more chair to our table?

可以加一張椅子嗎？

How about that one in the quiet corner or by the window?

在安靜角落或者靠近窗口的那張桌子怎麼樣？

帶位 Seating Guests

This way please.	請這邊走。
Could you follow me, please?	請跟我來,好嗎？
I'll show you to your table.	我帶你到座位。
Let me take you to the table near the window.	讓我帶你到靠近窗口的桌子。
Would you please come with me?	請跟我來，好嗎？

詢問顧客是否對座位滿意 Asking Guests If Happy With the Seats

Is this OK?	這張桌子可以嗎？
Will this be fine?	這座位好嗎？
Perfect! Let's take it.	太好了，我就要這位置。
I don't care for this table.	我不喜歡這張桌子。
I don't like that table in a poor position.	那張桌子的位置不好，我不喜歡。
Take a seat please. I'll be right back.	請坐，我馬上就回來。
Have a seat please. I'll be with you in a few minutes. 請坐，我一會兒就回來。	

請求客人等待座位 Asking Guests to Wait for Seats

How long do you think we will have to wait?

您認為我們還要等多久？

I'll wait for the table by the window, please call me when it is available.

我想等窗邊那張桌子，如果空出來了請通知我。

Sorry about the delay. Thank you for waiting.

抱歉讓您久等了。謝謝！

The table is ready now, this way please.

有位置了，這邊請。

We can't seat you at the same table at this moment.

我們現在不能讓你們同坐在一起。

We don't have a table for eight now, but there will be one after about 20 minutes, do you mind waiting in the lounge?

現在沒有能坐8個人的餐桌，要等大概20分鐘才有。您們願意到休息室等嗎？

Would you mind sharing the table with other people?

你是否願意與其它人一起坐？

Would you mind sitting separately?

你願意（介意）分開坐嗎？

Would you mind waiting until it is free or would you prefer another table?

您介意等一會兒嗎？或者您去另外一桌好嗎？

Would you mind waiting until the next table is available?

你介意（是否願意）等待下一個座位嗎？

Your reserved table will need another minute before it's ready.

你預訂的座位還要幾分鐘才可以好。

I. 基礎篇 Basic Expressions

與客人聊天 Chatting with Guests

Can you speak mandarin or Cantonese?

你可以講國語或廣東話嗎？

Do you cook yourself at home?

你在家自己做飯嗎？

Do you like to travel?

你喜歡旅游嗎？

Have you ever been to China?

你有去過中國嗎？

How many languages can you speak?

你可以講幾種語言？

How often do you have Chinese food?

你多久吃一次中國菜？

How old is she? 她多大了？

How was your China Trip? 中國旅行怎麼樣？

How's business going? 生意怎麼樣？

I haven't seen you for a while, how is everything?

我們已經很久沒見您了，最近怎樣？

It is cold outisde, today. 今天外面很冷。

Once a week，sometimes twice. 每周一次，有時兩次。

What a cute baby! Is it a girl or boy?

這小孩多可愛! 是女的還是男的？

What kind of food do you like? 你喜歡哪種菜？

Who take care of your baby while you're working?

你上班時誰照顧這小孩？

點菜
Taking Orders

服務客人 Serving Guests

呈遞菜單 Presenting A Menu

Here is the menu. Take your time, please.	這是菜單，請慢慢來。
I'll be right back to take your order.	我馬上回來點你的菜。
Let me have a look at the menu first.	讓我先看看菜單。
May I bring you something to drink?	您需要喝點什麼嗎？
May I have a menu please?	可以給我一個菜單嗎？
May I take a look at the menu first?	我可以先看看菜單嗎？
Would you like hot tea or iced water?	你喜歡熱茶還是冰水？

可以點菜 Ready to Order

Are you ready sir?	你準備好了嗎，先生？
Are you ready to order now?	你現在可以準備點菜了嗎？
Excuse me, sir. May I take your order now? 打擾一下，先生，您現在可以點菜了嗎？	
Have you chosen something already?	你已經選好了菜嗎？

點菜 Taking Orders

Do you need any wine with your meal?	用餐時，要一些酒嗎？
How many sodas do you want?	你們要多少個汽水？
Let me start with 2 wonton soups.	讓我先要兩碗餛飩湯。
What about you, sir?	你呢，先生？

21

I.基礎篇 Basic Expressions

What kind of juice would you prefer?

你比較喜歡哪種果汁？

What would you like to begin with?

你要先吃什麼？

What would you like to order?

你想點什麼？

Would anyone like a drink to start with?

有人先要飲料嗎？

Would you care for some soups?

你要一些湯嗎？

Would you like something to drink?

要一些喝的嗎？

還要別的嗎？ Anything else?

Anything else?	還要別的嗎？
I think it's enough.	我想這些應該夠了。
I think that is enough.	我想已經夠了。
That is all for now.	現在就這些。
That'll do it for today.	今天就這些了。
That's all.	就這些了。
That's everything.	就這些了。
That's it.	就這些。
Will that be it for now?	現在就這些？

推薦
Recommendations

詢問 Inquiry

Do you have any dishes for Vegetarian?

您們有沒有素食餐？

Do you have any dishes without meat?

有沒有什麼菜裏面沒有肉的？

Do you use M.S.G？ I'm allergic to it.

你們用味精嗎? 我會過敏的。

Does it come with any soup？ 它配湯嗎？

Excuse me. That's no "sauce" or no "salt"?

對不起，不要"醬汁"還是不要"鹽"？

How big is a quarter？ Is it enough for two people?

一誇脫有多大，它夠兩個人吃嗎？

How do you like your food made？ 你喜歡你的菜怎麼個做法？

How do you prepare it？ 怎樣烹調？

How many pieces come in a small order of spare ribs?

小份量的排骨有多少條的？

I mean: hot, mild or whatever you want.

我意思是：要棘的、一點辣的或其它。

Is General Tso's Chicken very hot？ 佐宗雞很辣嗎？

It depends on how many you can eat. 這要看你能吃多少。

Let me double check with the chef and come back．

讓我和廚師核對一下就回來。

I. 基礎篇 Basic Expressions

Let me show you. This is a pint, this is a quart.

讓我給你看，這是一品脫，那是一誇脫。

May I ask a question, please?

我可以問一個問題嗎？

No more lobster. It's all sold out.　沒有龍蝦了，全都賣完了。

No, actually we don't use any M. S. G. at all.

不，實際上我們根本不用味精。

Not very，but we can make it as hot as you want it.

不是很辣，但是我們可以根據你的要求做出辣度。

Small has 4 pieces, large has 8 pieces.

小份量的排骨有四條，大份量的有八條。

The Chef can leave out the M.S.G.　廚師可以不放味精。

We use M. S. G. in some dishes only.

我們祇在一些菜式上放味精。

What kind of sauce is in the Seafood Delight?

海鮮大雜燴含用什麼醬汁？

What's included in the lunch special?

特別午餐包括什麼？

What's your chef's specialty today?

今天廚師的特別菜是什麼？

Yes，many under "diet food".

有的，很多都在"低熱量食物"部份。

You just tell me if you don't like it.

如果你不要，祇要告訴我一聲。

If you are in hurry, I would recommend…

如果您趕時間，我推薦您…

味道介紹 Flavor Introductions

常用短語 Useful Phrases

A little bit hot	一點點辣	Not too much broccoli	不要太多芥蘭
A lot of pepper	多青椒	Plain fried rice	齋炒飯（不加任何東西）
Add an extra $4 of beef	多加四塊錢的牛肉		
Chicken instead of beef	鷄肉代替牛肉	Put the sauce separately	醬汁分開放
Extra scallion	多一點葱	Sauce on the side	醬汁另外放
How many pieces?	多少條/塊？		
Just a little hot	祇是一點點辣		
More onion	多洋葱	Separate sauce　醬汁分開	
No garlic sauce	不用蒜汁	With garlic sauce　用蒜汁	
No M.S.G	不要味精	With no ice　不要冰塊	
Not hot	不要辣的	Without M.S.G.　不要味精	
Not too greasy	不要太油	Without oil　不要油	

介紹 套餐 Introducing Set Meals

Does it come with any soup?	它有配湯嗎？
I don't want soup, just extra fried rice.	不要湯，祇要多點炒飯。
It comes with rice.	它配有米飯。
Ok, I'll make a note of it.	讓我做個記號。
Pork fried rice instead of white rice.	叉燒飯代替白飯。
What comes with it?	它配什麼？
What goes with the lunch box?	午餐盒配什麼？

25

I. 基礎篇 Basic Expressions

要求 Request

Can you make fried rice instead of white rice?

可以用炒飯代替白飯嗎？

Could I have ice in a separate glass?

我能在另外的杯子裏加冰嗎？

Could we have just a little sugar in the coffee?

我們可以在咖啡裏加點糖嗎？

Could you ask him to go easy on the salt?

您能讓他少放鹽嗎？

Do you have any gluten-free meals? 您們有不含面筋的菜嗎？

Do you want an extra plate? 您想再要一個盤嗎？

Don't forget to put the sauce separately. 請不要忘了把醬汁分開。

I can't have anything with dairy products. 我不吃任何有奶制品的東西。

I don't want any onion in my rice. 我的炒飯裏不要洋葱。

I don't want it too greasy. 我不想讓這道菜油太多了。

I don't need noodles. Is it the same price? 我不要緬條，一樣價格嗎？

I don't think so. 我不這樣認爲。

I'm allergic to tomatoes. 我對西紅柿過敏。

I've got a nut allergy. 我不吃堅果。

I'm afraid you'll pay an extra $2 for it. 恐怕你要多付二塊錢。

I'm in a hurry, could you make it quickly？ 我趕時間，你能做快一點嗎？

Is it possible to make it with white sauce? 有可能用白醬汁嗎？

Is it too late to change my mind？ 改變主意已經太遲了嗎？

Make the sauce light, broccoli soft， please.

醬汁做淡一點，芥蘭燒嫩一點。

May I add something to my order? 我可以在我單子裏加點東西嗎?

May I have extra chicken in it? 我可以加一些雞肉嗎?

Please don't add too much oil. 請不要加太多的油。

Please hold the food; we still have one friend coming.

請稍後上菜,我們還有一個朋友沒到。

Spare ribs well-done, but not burnt,please.

排骨烤熟一點,但不要燒焦。

Sure, no problem, just as you like.

當然設有問題,隨你喜歡。

There isn't any meat in this dish.

這道菜裏沒有肉。

This is too oily.

這個太油膩了。

We are not used to spicy food. Please don't put any chili in the meal.

我們不太習慣辣味食物。請不要放辣椒。

We can make many flavors to suit you.

我們可做多種風味來適合你。

We have vegetarian-friendly meals on our menu.

我們的菜單上有適合素食者的菜。

We would like something delicious in typical Chinese style.

我們想要有中國風味的美食。

We'd like to share this meal.

我們想共享這道菜。

Would you like it on the side?

配菜您想點這個嗎?

I.基礎篇 Basic Expressions

推薦 Recommendations

Are you on a special diet? 你有特別節食嗎？

Could you have something else, instead? 你能點其它的嗎？

Did you ever try Happy Family before? 你以前曾經試過全家福嗎？

Have you ever eaten sesame Chicken before? 你曾吃過芝麻雞嗎？

How about our chef's special? 我們廚師的特別菜怎麼樣？

I am not familiar with Chinese food, could you recommend something?

我對中國菜不熟悉，您能不能推薦一下？

I would suggest something different for you.

我為你推薦一些不同的菜式。

I'm a vegetarian. 我是吃素的。

I'm afraid it is not enough for four persons. It would be better to add two dishes.

恐怕這不夠4個人食用，加多兩道菜比較好。

I'm sorry, eggplant is out of season. 對不起，茄子已經過季了。

That one is not on the menu, but we can make one special for you.

那個在菜單上設有，但是我們可以特地為您做一份。

That would be to your taste. 那將很適合你的味口。

The set course will not take as much time. I would recommend that you order a set course for two persons. It is cheap and delicious.

套餐不會花那麼長時間。我推薦您點兩份的套餐，即經濟又實惠。

The spinach is in season now. Would you like to try it?

菠菜剛剛上市，您想嘗試一下嗎？

This big portion is suitable for three of you.

這個大份量很適合你們三個人。

This course is for a minimum of 5 to 6 persons. I think the portions will be too large for two.

這道菜至少是5到6個人吃的，我想這對兩個人來說太多了。

What kind of meat would you prefer? 你比較喜歡哪種肉？

What would you like to order? 你（們）想點些什麽？

Why don't you order a set course? 你們爲什麽不點一份套餐？

Would you like your crabs steamed or fried with ginger and spring onion?

您要的大蟹是清蒸還是姜葱炒？

You can choose either chicken，beef or shrimp.

你可以從鷄肉、牛肉、蝦中選一種。

You have a choice of either soup or soda for an extra $0.3 only.

你可以選擇湯或汽水，祇要另加三毛錢。

解釋菜品 Describing Dishes

Generally speaking, Cantonese cuisine is light and clear; Sichuan cuisine is strong and hot; Shanghai cuisine is oily and Beijing cuisine is spicy and a bit salty. 一般來説，粵菜比較清淡，川菜濃烈而辛辣，上海菜比較油，而京菜較香而咸。

The Chicken Soup with Cream Corn is the soup with corn and minced chicken. It is sweet and delicious.

鷄茸玉米羹是用甜玉米和鷄茸做的，很鮮甜。

The stewed mutton is stewed in wine with carrot, onion.

炖羊肉是用葡萄酒炖的，還配有蘿卜和洋葱。

Would you tell me how the "steamed pork wrapped with rice flour" is cooked? 您能告訴我們粉蒸肉是怎麽做的嗎？

I. 基礎篇 Basic Expressions

How many ways are there to cook chicken? 請問您們有多少種方法煮雞？

How do you cook it? 這道菜怎麼做的？

It looks good, smells good and tastes good. 這道菜色，香，味俱全。

It's very popular among our guests. 它非常受歡迎。

It's a well-known delicacy in Chinese cuisine.

它是中國菜的一道有名的佳肴。

What is the best way to cook scallops? 請問用什麼方法烹制扇貝最好？

推薦餐前酒 Aperitif Recommendations

Could you recommend some good wine? 可否推薦一些不錯的酒？

I'd like to have French red wine. 我想要喝法國紅酒。

I'd like to have some local wine. 我想點當地出產的酒。

May I order a glass of wine? 我可以點杯酒嗎？

May I see the wine list? 可否讓我看看酒單？

Rice wine goes perfectly with crabs. 喝米酒吃螃蟹是絕對的美味。

Since you are in a Chinese restaurant now, we would recommend the Chinese wine.

既然您們在中國餐廳裏，我建議您們試試中國酒。

Since you ordered the Sashimi, I'd suggest Japanese Sake to go with your meal. 既然您們點了刺身，我建議您試試日本青酒。

What kind of drinks do you have for an aperitif? 您想點些什麼餐前酒嗎？

What kind of wine do you have? 你有哪幾類酒？

Would you care for something stronger? 您想來點度數高一點的酒嗎？

Would you like a aperitif with your meal? 您要點佐餐酒嗎？

Would you like a bottle of red wine to go with your beef?

要不要來瓶紅葡萄酒來配您的牛扒？

上菜用語 Serving Dishes

And appetizer to follow. 接下來的是開胃小吃。

Another egg roll is coming soon. 另外一個春卷馬上就好了。

Do you want me to serve it now or later? 現在上菜還是等會？

Excuse me, sir. May I serve the dishes now?
打擾一下先生，請問可以上菜了嗎？

Have I served you everything by now? 現在你們的菜都齊了嗎？

Here is your food. Please enjoy it. 這是您點的菜，請慢用！

I hope all of you enjoy your food. 希望你們盡情享用。

Is it time to serve you the main dishes? 現在可以上主菜了嗎？

Just let me know if you need any help. 如果有什麼需要，請告訴我。

May I have a cup of coffee before my food is ready?
在我的菜好之前請給我一杯咖啡好嗎？

May I make room for this dish? 我可以整理一個位置來放這一盤嗎？

Please enjoy! 請慢用。（上完最後一道菜時說的）

The Chinese way is to serve the soup first and then the food; if you like, we'll bring you the food first. 按中國的方式，是先上湯再上菜；如果您喜歡，我們可以先上菜再上湯。

The other dishes need a while. 其它的菜要等一會兒。

The soup is ready, please enjoy！ 湯已經盛好了，請慢用！

This is very hot. Please be careful. 這道菜很燙，請小心。

Would you like us to serve the dishes now? 可以上菜了嗎？

Would you like your rice now or later? 是現在為您裝飯還是遲一些？

You have ordered two main dishes. Would you like to serve them together or separately? 您點了兩道主菜，請問是一起上還是分開上？

提供幫助 Offering Help

Bring me a high chair please when you have a chance.

有空時請給我一張高椅子（小孩椅子）。

Can you wipe the table for me, please?

你能幫我擦一下桌子好嗎？

May I bring you a knife and a folk? It seems you are not used to chopsticks.

看來您不太習慣用筷子，需要我給您拿一副刀叉嗎？

May I change the plate for you?

可以爲你換碟嗎？

May I have another one when you have a chance?

有空時請給我另外一個。

May I have one more spoon?

我能多要個勺子嗎？

May I take the glass away?

我可以將杯子拿着嗎？

The room is too cold, could you turn up the air-conditioning?

房間太冷了，可以把空調調高一點嗎？

Will you change the table cloth, please?

請你幫我換一個桌布好嗎？

Will you clean the table, please? 你能幫我收拾一下桌子嗎？

Will you give me some more napkins, please? 請多給我一些餐巾好嗎？

Will you pass the salt shaker for me? 請把鹽瓶遞給我好嗎？

Would you please bring us one extra chair please?

可以幫我們多拿一張椅子嗎？

Would you please separate the fish for us? 可以幫忙把魚分一分嗎？

詢問正在用餐顧客的意見 Asking for Opinion

Are you enjoying your meal? 你們吃得開心嗎?

Do you know how to use chopsticks? 你知道怎樣用筷子嗎?

Do you like it? 你喜歡嗎?

Do you need any help? 您需要幫忙嗎?

How are the dishes? 這些菜怎樣?

How is the fish? 魚怎麼樣?

I hope all of you enjoy your food. 希望你們盡情享用。

If you need anything else, just feel free to tell me.
如果您還需要別的什麼,盡管告訴我好了。

Is it OK? 不錯嗎?

Just let me know if you need any help. 如需要幫忙,請告訴我。

Let me show you how to practice. 請讓我示範給你看怎樣用。

Should I change this plate with a smaller one?
我把這個換成小一點的碟子,好嗎?

Some more rice? 要添飯嗎?

Thank you for pointing out our shortcomings, we'll try our best to make improvements. 謝謝您指出我們的不足,我們會盡力改善的。

The dishes are very delicious, but the service is not satisfactory enough.
菜品做的不錯,但是服務質量不夠好。

There is still some soup left. Would anyone care for some?
還有一些湯,請問哪位客人需要添加?

Was it good? 好嗎?

What else can I do for you? 我還能幫你做什麼嗎?

Would you care for more hot tea? 你們再來些熱茶怎麼樣?

33

I.基礎篇 Basic Expressions

餐後甜點 Serving Dessert

Are you ready for dessert? 你準備要甜點了嗎?

Could you wrap it up for me, please? 請幫我把它包起來好嗎?

Do you have any jelly? 你們有果凍甜點嗎?

Do you want it to go? 你要打包帶走嗎?

Have you finished yet? 你吃好了嗎?

Just leave it here. I'll take care of that. 就放在那裏，我會處理的。

May I clear the table for you? 我可以為您收拾桌子嗎?

May I take the empty plates away now? 現在我可以把空盤子拿走嗎?

This is the complete course. There is a dessert to follow.
全部的菜已經上齊了，接下來還有甜點。

When shall I bring you dessert? 我什麼時候給你上甜點?

Would you like some dessert? 您要來點兒甜品嗎?

埋單結帳 Paying the Bills

Can I have the bill, please? 請結賬。

 Just a moment, please. The cashier will have your bill ready in a minute.
請稍等，收銀員馬上會準備好您的賬單。

How would you like to pay for the meal?

請問您打算用什麼方式結賬?

Would you like separate bills or one bill?

請問是分開結賬還是一起結賬?

Would you like to pay separately or together?

請問是分開結賬還是一起結賬?

May I know who is paying, please? 請問是哪位付賬？

I'll take care of the bill. 我來付這個賬單。

Would you like a breakdown of the bill?

您的賬面要細分嗎？

Do you accept Credit Cards and Personal Check?

您們收取信用卡和個人支票嗎？

I am sorry, but we don't accept personal checks.

對不起，我們不接受個人支票。

We'd like to split the bill.

我們想平攤賬單。

We only accept the credit cards displayed.

我們祇接受在這裏的信用卡。

Sorry, we don't accept credit card or check.

對不起，我們不收信用卡和支票。

What's the expiration date?

信用卡的有效期是什麼時候？

Whose check shall I put the soda on?

我應該將汽水記到誰的賬單上呢？

Do I pay you or the cashier?

是在這兒結賬還是在櫃臺結帳？

You can pay the cashier at the counter as you go out.

出去時，可以在櫃臺收銀員那裏付錢。

You may pay at the table.

你就在桌面上付錢就可以了。

May I have a Receipt for this meal?

我可以要一份這餐的賬單嗎？

35

I. 基礎篇 Basic Expressions

提醒客人結帳 Reminding Customers to Pay the Bills

Excuse me, sir. Our last order is at 10 o'clock. Would you like something else?
對不起先生，我們的收餐時間是10點鐘，請問您還要點什麼嗎？

Would you like anything else, madam? It is nearly our last order time.
我們最後點菜的時間快到了，請問還需要點什麼嗎？

Our buffet will close in 30 minutes. If you want anything more, please get it as soon as possible.
對不起，還有30分鐘自助餐就收餐了。如果您還需要點什麼，請早點取用。

Excuse me, sir. Do you need anything else? If not, do you mind if I bring you the bill? It is nearly closing time.
對不起，先生。請問您還需要點什麼嗎？如果不需要的話，介不介意先結賬呢？因為我們打烊的時間就要到了。

Excuse me, sir, would you like to sign the bill now? I'm really sorry to have delayed you. 對不起，先生，您是否願意現在結賬呢？耽誤您的時間，真是不好意思。

May I prepare the bill for you now, madam?
請問，我現在可以問您準備賬單嗎？

結賬出錯 Mistakes on Bills

Here is the money you overpaid. 您多付的錢。

Here is the right change. 這是如數的零錢。

How much change did I give you before? 剛才我給你多少零錢？

How much did I charge you before? 剛才，我算你多少錢？

I think you charged me too much.

我想你算了我太多錢。

I'm afraid there are a 15% service charge and 8.75% sale tax.

恐怕還得加上15%服務費和8.75%銷售稅。

I'm awfully sorry. The cashier miscalculated the bill by adding the bill on the other tables to yours.

真對不起，收銀員把您鄰桌的賬單記到您的賬單上了。

I'm sorry about that.

為此我感到萬分抱歉。

I'm sorry to hear that. I'll double check.

很抱歉聽到您這麼說。我去核對一下。

If you think there is anything wrong in your bill, we can check it for you.

如果您認為賬目有錯，我們可以為您核對一下。

I'm afraid you overcharged me.

恐怕你多收了我的錢。

Is anything wrong with your change?

找給你的錢有錯嗎？

One of the beers should have been deducted from your bill.

其中一份啤酒應該從您的賬單中扣除。

That's much more than I expected.

那比我想象中要超出許多呢。

We will correct your bill be deducting $28.00 from the total.

我們將把賬單改過來，從總額中減去$28。

Your bill includes a 10% service charge and a 8% sale tax.

您的賬單包括10%的服務費和8%的銷售稅。

I. 基礎篇 Basic Expressions

送客 Farewell

Have a nice evening. 祝您有個愉快的夜晚。

Have you taken all your belongings?
您的物品都帶齊了嗎？

I hope you enjoyed your dinner. Please come again.
希望您用餐愉快。歡迎請再次光臨。

If anything is wrong, please tell us.
若有不到之處，請告訴我們。

If you enjoy your stay, please tell your friends.
若覺得滿意，請告訴您的朋友。

It's my pleasure to serve you and your family.
能招待你和你的家人，這是我的榮幸。

Please say Hello to your family.
請代我向你家人問好。

Thank you for dining with us.
謝謝你在我們這裏用餐。

We all look forward to serving you again.
真誠期待再次爲您服務。

We hope to see you again soon.
我們希望能快再見到你。

We're very happy to serve you.
我很高興接待你。

Would you like me to call a taxi for you?
請問您需要我幫您叫出租車嗎？

You have a good weekend. 祝周末愉快。

II. 外賣餐館
Takeout Restaurants

- ☑ 接單常用短語 Common Phrases While Taking Orders
- ☑ 電話接單常用句子

    Common Sentences for Taking Orders on the Phone
- ☑ 指示方向的常用語 Common Phrases in Directions
- ☑ 外賣餐館情景對話

    Situational Dialogues at Take-out Restaurants
- ☑ 外賣接單 Take Out Orders
- ☑ 送餐寫地址實況會話 Delivery Conversations
- ☑ 櫃枱接單會話 Taking Orders at the Counter

II.外賣餐館 Takeout Restaurants

接單常用短語 Common Phrases While Taking Orders

我能幫你嗎？ May I help you?

Can I help you, miss?	我能幫您忙嗎，小姐？
Have you been helped?	您已經接待了嗎？
How may I help you?	我能爲您做什麼呢？
May I help you, sir?	我能幫您忙嗎，先生？
May I take your order?	我可以爲您下單嗎？
Next, please.	請下一位。

要求一個菜單 Request for a Menu

Can I have a look at the menu?	我可以看看菜單嗎？
Do you have a lunch menu?	你有午餐菜單嗎？
Here it is.	在這裏。
May I have a menu please?	我可以要一個菜單嗎？
May I have a takeout menu?	我可以要一份外賣的菜單嗎？
Where is the menu?	菜單在哪裏？

請慢慢來 Take Your Time

Give me a couple of minutes, please.	請給我一些時間。
I don't know yet.	我還不知道。
Let me know when you are ready.	你準備好了，請讓我知道。
Take your time please.	請慢慢來。

我要…… I Want…..

Circle what you want please.	請圈上你所要的。

Could you circle your order on the menu?	可以在菜單上畫上您要點的菜嗎？
I want to order a quart of beef Lo Mein.	我要訂一誇脱牛肉撈面。
I want two pints of chicken & broccoli.	我要二品脱芥蘭鷄。
Let me have one combination dinner.	我要一個特別晚餐。
Mark it on the menu please.	請在菜單上標明（你所要的）。
May I have a No. 2 lunch special?	我可以要一個2號特別午餐嗎？
Please give me one order of Happy Family.	請給我一份全家福。

可以點菜了　Ready to Order

Are you ready to order?	你準備好點菜了嗎？
Are you ready, Sir?	你準備好了嗎，先生？
May I take your order now?	你現在可以點菜了嗎？
Would you like to order now?	你現在可以點菜了嗎？

分量　Size

Can or bottle?	鐵罐的還是瓶裝的？
One liter or two liters?	小罐還是大罐？
Pint or quart?	是品脱（16安士）還是誇脱（32安士）？
Small or large?	小的還是大的？
What size?	要多大的？

帶走還是在這裏吃 For Here or To Go

Take out or eat in?	外賣還是堂吃？
For here or to go?	這裏吃還是帶走？
For pick-up or delivery?	來拿還是送餐？

II. 外賣餐館 Takeout Restaurants

Take home or stay here? 外賣還是這裏吃？

Take out or eat here? 外賣還是在這裏吃？

To be picked up or delivered? 是來拿還是送餐？

Would you like to come in and pick it up or have it delivered?
您是願意來取還是我們給您送？

Delivery is free for orders over $10.00. 點菜$10.00以上的免費送餐。

It must be within five miles of our restaurant.
一定要在離我們餐廳5英裏以內的地方。

Our drivers don't carry cash with them. 我們的司機不帶現金。

訂菜號碼 Order Numbers

Here is your order number.	這是你訂菜的號碼。
Here is your ticket number.	這是你訂菜號碼。
Keep your ticket please.	請拿着你的號碼。
Wait until your number is called.	請稍候，我會叫你的號碼。
We will call your order number.	我們將叫您的定單號碼。

多少錢 How Much

How much? 多少錢？	It's $40.00 even. 它是四十元整。
How much does it come to?	That would be $7.15. 它是 $7.15
總計多少錢？(come to：總計)	It comes to $32.85. 總計 $32.85
How much do I owe you? 多少錢？	The total is $46.00 總共是$46.00.
How much is it altogether? 總共多少錢？	They only accept exact change.
What's the total? 總額多少？	他們祇接受正好的錢。

現在付錢還是待會付 Pay Now or Later

Do you accept credit cards?	你們有收信用卡嗎？
Do you take personal checks?	你們有收私人支票嗎？
Either way.	兩種都可以。
Now is fine.	現在付可以。
One check or two?	一個賬單還是分兩個賬單？
Pay now or later?	現在付錢還是待會付錢？
Pay together or separately?	一起算還是分開算？
Same bill or separate bill?	一起付還是分開付？
We only accept Cash.	我們祇收現金。
Whatever you like.	隨便你喜歡。
You may pay now.	你可以現在付。

多長時間 How Long

How long? 多長時間？	About 10 minutes.	大概十分鐘。
How long will it take?	Just a couple of minutes.	祇要幾分鐘。
要花多少時間？	Just a few minutes.	祇要幾分鐘。
When will it be ready?	How much longer?	還要多長時間？
多長時間可以做好？		

馬上回來 Be Right Back

I'll be right back.	我馬上回來。
I'll be back in ten minutes.	我十分鐘回來。
I'll come back to pick it up.	我將回來拿菜。
I'll wait.	我在等。

II. 外賣餐館 Takeout Restaurants

快要好了 Almost Ready

Almost ready. 快要好了。	Is it done? 它好了嗎？
Almost done. 快要好了。	Is my order ready yet?
It is coming soon. 馬上就好了。	我的菜好了嗎？
It's not ready yet. 它還沒好。	We're still working on it.
Just a minute, please. 再要一分鐘就好了。	我們正在做你的菜。
	Still one more thing. 還有一個菜（就好了）。

你們還提供午餐嗎？ Do you still serve lunch?

Do you still serve lunch?	你們還提供午餐嗎？
Is the lunch time still on?	還有午餐嗎？
The lunch time is over.	午餐時間過去了。
Did I catch the lunch time?	我趕得上午餐時間嗎？
It's 3.00 PM now; lunch time is finished. 現在是下午三點了，午餐時間已經過了。	
OK! We'll make one for you. 那好！我們做一個午餐給你。	

櫃臺出菜 Serving Food at the Counter

一起還是分開裝 Put It Together or Separately

Same bag or separate bag?	裝在一起還是分開裝？
Put it together or separately?	一起放還是分開放？
May I have a plastic bag?	請給我一個塑料袋？
Please mark what is inside each bag.	請註明每個膠袋裏面是什麼。

出菜時的幾種叫法 Serving Expressions

Excuse me, sir! It's all set.	喂，先生，你的菜好了。
Yes madam! Your order is ready.	太太，你的菜好了。
Phone number 718-987-6543	電話號碼 718–987-6543
Ticket # 3210　訂菜號碼# 3210	Is Edison here?　愛迪生在嗎？

這就是你的訂單 Here is your order

Here you go.　這就是你的（訂菜）。	Here is your order. 這就是您的訂單。
Here it is, Miss. 這就是你的，小姐。	Thank you for waiting.
Here you are.　這就是你的。	謝謝你的等待。

你要哪種醬汁？ What kind of Sauce?

What kind of sauce, sir?	（你要）哪種醬汁，先生？
Forks and spoons are over there.	餐叉和湯匙在那避。
Help yourself to the sauce please.	您自己拿調味汁。
Take some sauce over there.	在那邊拿點調味汁。
No, I'm all set. Thanks.	不用了，這樣就好了，謝謝。
Do you need a bag for soda?	你要一個袋來裝汽水嗎？

一切都齊了 Everything is inside

Everything is inside.	一切都齊了（都在裏面了）。
Are you sure everything is here?	你肯定都齊了嗎？
Let me double check.	讓我小心查一查。

請這樣拿 Hold it like this

Hold it like this please. 這樣拿。	Hold it this way please. 請這樣拿。

II. 外賣餐館 Takeout Restaurants

Hold the bottom please.	請托下面。	Keep flat please.	請保持平衡。
Keep straight when you put it in your car. 放在車的時候，請保持直着放。			

詢問櫃臺前的客人 Have you been helped?

Are you picking up?	你是來拿菜的嗎？
Did you call in or order here?	你是打電話來還是在這裏訂菜？
Have you been helped?	你已經接待了嗎？
I called in my order.	我打電話訂了菜（我來拿菜之意）。
May I help someone?	有人要幫忙嗎？
What's your order (number), sir?	你的菜（號碼）是什麼？
Yes?	我可以幫你嗎？（較隨便的問法）

告別語 Saying good-bye

Bye now.	再見。	Enjoy your lunch.	享用你的午餐。
See you next time.	下次見。	See you soon.	很快見到你。
You have a good day.	祝你有愉快的一天。	You too.	你也是。

電話接單常用句子
Common Sentences for Taking Orders on the Phone

接電話 Answering Phone

Buffet King, may I help you?	自助王，我能幫你忙嗎？
Great Wall, can I help you?	長城，我能幫你忙嗎？
Yellow River, how can I help you?	黃河，我能幫你嗎？

下外賣菜單 Placing Delivery Orders

I want to order something to go.	我要訂一些外買。
I'd like to place an order for pick up.	我要訂菜，自己來拿。
I'd like to place an order for delivery.	我要訂一些外送的菜。
I want to make an order to take out.	我要訂外賣菜。
May I order some food for delivery?	我可以訂一些外送的菜嗎？
I'd like to place an order.	我想點餐。

電話號碼 Phone Number

Your phone number and address please?	請問你的電話號碼和地址？
What's your phone number?	你的電話號碼是什麼？
What's your telephone number?	您的電話號碼是多少？
May I have your name please?	請問您叫什麼名字？
Could you tell me your name please?	你能告訴我你的名字嗎？
It's 626-321-7654.	它是626－321-7654。
What is your address?	您的地址是？
What is your house number?	您的房間號是什麼？
What street is it on?	在哪條街上？
Is that near the Subway station?	離地鐵站近嗎？
It is on the third flights of stairs.	在三樓。

請等一下 Hold on Please

Hold on please. 請稍等一下	Hold on one moment please. 請等一會兒。
Would you hold the line please? 請你等一會兒好嗎？	
Hang on one second please. 請等一會兒。	
Thank you for waiting. 謝謝你的等待。	Go ahead please! 請繼續講吧！

II. 外賣餐館 Takeout Restaurants

要求再說一遍 Please Repeat

Excuse me! Could you please repeat? 對不起，可以再說一遍嗎？

Forget about it. 算了。

I beg your pardon! What did you say? 不好意思，你剛才說什麼了？

Never mind. 算了。

Pardon me! Would you please speak louder? 不好意思，可以大聲點嗎？

Sorry I can't hear you. 對不起，我聽不見。

Sorry, can you say it again please? 對不起，請再說一遍。

Would you speak a little bit louder please? 請你講大聲一點好嗎？

Would you speak slowly please? 請你講慢一點好嗎？

確認菜單 Confirming Orders

Could you start all over again, please? 你能再從頭開始嗎？

I'd like to confirm your order. 我想確認一下您點的餐。

Let me repeat your order. 讓我重復一遍你的菜。

Let's confirm the order. 讓我們確認一下訂單。

May I read it back to make sure? 我可以念一遍來確認一下嗎？

Yeah. I got everything. 是的，我都記下來了。

Yes, I got it. 是的，我懂了。 | You got that? 你懂了嗎？

在菜單上的號碼 The Number on the Menu

Could you tell me the number? 你能告訴我它的號碼嗎？

I couldn't find it. 我找不到它。

I have no menu in front of me. 我面前沒有菜單。

I'm new here. 我是新來的。

Is it a lunch special or regular order? 是特別午餐還是一般的菜？

It's under "Seafood" Section.	它在海鮮那欄。
It's at the bottom of the menu.	它在菜單的下面。
It's on the chef's special menu。	它在厨師特別菜菜單上。
What's the number on this menu?	它在菜單上是幾號？
Would you order by number please?	請用號碼來點菜好嗎？

拿菜的時間 Time to Pick Up

I'll be there at 6:45.	我6點45分到那裏。
I'll pick it up at ten after eight (8:10).	我八點十分來拿菜。
I'll be down there shortly (immediately).	我很快到那裏。
I won't be there until 8 o'clock.	我八點才到那裏。
I won't pick it up till noon.	我中午才來拿菜。
I'm going to be there soon.	我將馬上到那裏。

詢問營業時間 Inquire Business Hours

Are you open on New Year's Day?	你們新年照常營業嗎？
Are you still open?	你們還營業嗎？
How late are you open till?	你們營業到什麼時候？
Last order for eating in is at 9:30.	堂吃的最後一個菜是9:30。
Sorry，we are closed.	對不起，我們關門了。
What time do you close?	你什麼時候關門？
Will you be here by 10:00?	你十點以前能來嗎？
We're open from 11:00AM to 10:30 PM．	早上11:00營業到晚上10:30。

II. 外賣餐館 Takeout Restaurants

跟進自取單 Follow Up on Pick Up Orders

Are you the same person I just talked to?
你就是剛才與我講話的那一位嗎？

I am calling from the Long River Chinese restaurant.
我是從長江中國餐館打來的。

I just want to make sure if someone is coming to pick up the order.
我祇想確定一下是否有人過來取。

Is someone on the way to pick it up? 是否有人來拿菜了？

Is this the same person who just called? 你就是剛才打電話的那一位碼？

May I speak to Mr. Smith? 我可以和史密斯先生通電話嗎？

He is on the way now. 他正在路上。

We will keep your food warm here. 我們會把你的菜保溫在這裏。

Will anybody be here any minute? 有人很快來拿菜嗎？

Your order has been ready for 15 minutes. 你的菜已經做好十五分鐘了。

没有人取訂單 Nobody Picks Up Order

Is this Mr. Johnson and phone number 917-876-5432?
請問是約翰遜及電話號碼917-876-5432嗎？

Your order is ready. 你的菜已經好了。

I didn't order any Chinese food. 我没訂任何中國菜。

I'm sorry to trouble (disturb) you. 對不起，打攪你了。

But someone ordered food and left this number.
但是有人訂了菜，并留下這個號碼。

菜熱好吃 Best eaten while it's hot

It's most tasty when it's just been made.　剛做的菜，味道最好。

It's best eaten while it's hot.	菜熱的時候最好吃。		
It will lose flavor if it sits too long.	放太久，會失去味道。		

指示方向的常用語
Common Phases in Directions

Side door	傍門、側門	Front door	前門
Back door	後門	Main gate	大門、前門
In front of building	在大樓前面	Behind you	在你後面
Between A and B	在A和B之間	At the corner	拐角處
Just around the corner	就在街角附近	It's pretty close	它們很近
Next to the bank	銀行隔壁	On the second floor	第二層
In the basement	在地下室	Across from A	在A的對面，橫遇A
Cross the street	越過街道	A is opposite B	A在B的對面

How to get there? 怎麼到那?

Walking	步行	By car	開車	By bicycle	騎自行車
Take a bus	乘巴士	Go ahead	向前走	Go straight ahead	直往前走

Go straight down the street	一直往這條街走下去
Go along the hall-way	沿着走廊直走
Keep going this way	往這條街走下去（上去）

All the way up	直往上走	Stay on Main street	繼續沿着緬街走

Walk four blocks until you get to…	走4個街區，直到您到了…
Walk up the stairs to 3/F.	從樓梯走到三樓.
Take the elevator to the top floor on your right when you get off the elevator.	乘電梯到頂樓走出電梯，就在你的右邊。

II. 外賣餐館 Takeout Restaurants

轉彎 Turning

Right turn 右轉	Left turn 左轉	Make a left turn 向左轉

Right turn at the second corner　第二個拐角處，右轉

Second turn on the left　第二個拐角處，左轉

爲開汽車指示方向 Offering Driving Directions

Drive to the side door	開到側門
Drive around to the back yard	開車繞到後院
Drive down three blocks and turn left.	直走三個街區，然後左轉。
Turn right after the first light.	過了第一個交通燈，向右轉。
Take exit 18 from the highway.	從高速公路18出口處出口。
Precede 4 0r 5 miles; you'll see a sign for the town.　繼續開4.5裏左右，你會找到去該城的招牌。	
It's easy to find it, you can't miss it.	那是很容易找到的，你不錯過的。
Which way is 7th Avenue?	哪一邊是第七大道？
Please show me on this map.	請在這地圖上指給我看。
I got lost on the way.	我迷路了。
I am m looking for a post office.	我正在我郵電局。
I am trying to find Main Street.	我正想找緬街。

拼寫地址的練習 Address Spelling Practice

A as in Apple	蘋果	B as in Boy	男孩
C as in Cat	猫	D as in Dog	狗
E as in Elephant	象	F as in Friend	朋友
G as in Girl	女孩	H as in Henry	亨利
I as in Ice Cream	冰淇淋	J as in John	約翰

K as in Kelly	凱利	L as in Linda	琳達
M as in Mary	瑪利	N as in Nancy	南希
O as in Open	開門	P as in Peter	彼得
Q as in Queen	女王	R as in Rose	玫瑰花
S as in Son	兒子	T as in Tony	湯尼
U as in Unit	單位	V as in Victory	勝利
W as in Water	水	X as in X-Ray	X-光
Y as in Yellow	黃色	Z as in Zebra	斑馬

請問有詢問送餐嗎？ Do you deliver?

Do you deliver?	你們送餐嗎？
Yes we do.	是的，我們有（送餐）。
Sorry we don't.	封不起，我們沒有（送餐）。
Free delivery.	免費送餐。
There's no delivery charge.	不收送餐費用。
The minimum order for delivery is $10.	最少10塊錢才送外賣。
It will be charged extra $1.	額外收費是一塊錢。
We deliver food within a 10-mile radius only.	我們祇送方圓10裏左右。

要送餐還是自己來拿 Delivered or Picked Up

It's for delivery, right?	這是送餐，對嗎？
Do you want it delivered or picked -up?	你是要送餐還是來拿？
Will that be delivery or picked up?	是送餐還是來拿？
Do you want us to send it over?	你要我們送過去嗎？
Could you send it up by 7 o'clock?	你能在七點前送來嗎？
Make it as soon as possible please.	請盡量快一點。
You said you wanted delivered, right?	你是說要送餐對嗎？

II. 外賣餐館 Takeout Restaurants

請問你的電話和地址 Phone Numbers and Addresses

May I have your address please?	我可以要你的地址嗎？
Your address and phone number, please?	請問你的地址和電話？
What's your address and Apt. number?	請問你的地址和公寓號碼？
I'm new around here.	我剛到這地區。
This place is strange to me.	我不熟悉這個地方。
May I have your detailed address?	我可以要個詳細的地址嗎？
I'm not familiar with Main Street.	我對緬街不熟悉。

拼寫 Spelling

How do you spell that?	怎麼拼寫？
Could you spell it for me please?	你能把它拼出來嗎？
Would you spell slowly please?	請你拼寫慢一點好嗎？
Excuse me, is it "G"or"J" ?	對不起，是G還是J？
"G" as in "girl", right?	女孩中的G，對嗎？
Is it "M" or "N",?	是M，還是N？
Is it letter "A" or number 8?	是字母"A"還是號碼中的"8"？
Would you mind spelling the word for me please?	你介意幫我拼寫嗎？

第幾層？ Which floor?

Where is your home?	你家在哪裏？
Where do you live?	你住在哪裏？
Where are you living?	你住在哪裏？
Which floor are you in?	你在第幾層？
What's your location?	你的地點在哪裏？
Where are you located?	你們座落在哪裏？

We are located in ABC plaza.	我們在ABC大廈。
Can you tell me where it is?	你可以告訴我在哪裏嗎？
Is it a private house or an Apartment building? 它是私家房還是公寓大樓?	

有多遠？ How far?

How far is it from here?	離這裏有多遠？
It's about 5 mile.	五裏左右。
How long will it take to get there?	到那裏要花多少時間？
It will take 5 minutes by car.	開車要五分鐘。
It's about two-minute walk.	走路大概兩分鐘。

怎樣到你家？ How can I go to your house?

How can I go to your house?	我怎樣去你的家？
How can I get to your Apt?	我怎樣到你的公寓？
Could you tell me how I can get there?	能告訴我怎樣到那兒嗎？
Would you give me directions please?	請給我一個指示好嗎？
Could you tell me the way to your place?	你能告訴我去你那個地方的路嗎？
What is the best way to get there?	到你那裏有什麽快捷方式嗎？

按門鈴 Ring the Bell

By the way, I want to break a fifty dollar bill. 順便提一下，我想換五十塊零錢。	
Give me a call before you leave.	離開之前給我一個電話。
I'll beep you down stairs.	我會在樓下按鈴。
I'll blow the car horn outside your house.	我會在你房子外面按喇叭。

II. 外賣餐館 Takeout Restaurants

Just knock on the door please. 請你敲一下門。

Please tell the delivery man to beep the horn. 請你告訴送餐人，按喇叭。

Press the door bell as soon as you get here. 你一到這裏就按門鈴。

We'll give you a call when we are going. 我們送去時，會給你打一個電話。

We'll leave the door open for you. 我將會把門開著。

When he arrives, just ring the bell. 他來的時候，祇要按一下鈴。

Will you have him bring enough change for that? 請要他帶足夠的零錢好嗎？

You can buzz me from the lobby. 你可在大廳按鈴通知我。

餐已經到達 Food is here

I'm delivering food for you; please open the door?
我是送餐給你的，請開門。

Please be downstairs in ten minutes.	十分鐘後，請到樓下。
Please go down to get it.	請下來拿。
Please go out to wait in ten-minutes.	十分鐘後，請出來等。
The guy is going to be there soon.	那小伙子很快就要到了。
This is the delivery man from Buffet King.	我是來自自助王送餐的。
Who are you looking for? 找誰？	Who is it? 請問誰？

Food hasn't come yet 餐還沒有送到

Could you wait a little longer please?	請你再多等一會兒可以嗎？
He is on the way.	他正在路上。
He should be there any minute.	他一會兒就到。
He should get to your house very soon.	他很快就會到你的家。
How come my food still hasn't come yet?	為什麼我的菜還沒來？

I am sorry to hear that, but we will do that for you.

很遺憾聽到那，但是我們會接受您的要求。

I called in my order more than half an hour ago. 我訂菜已經超過半小時。

I want to cancel my order. 我想取消我的訂菜。

I've been expecting my food for a long time. 我等好久了。

I'm very sorry for the delay. You'll receive a 10% off on your next order.

我很抱歉耽擱了時間。下次我們會給您10%的折扣。

I've been waiting for at least 30 minutes. 我最少等了三十分鐘了。

Let me check with the Chef right now. 我馬上查一查。

May I have your name and phone number again please?

請再説一次你的名字和電話。

Sorry for the inconvenience. 很抱歉給您帶來不便。

The delivery man left here 15 minutes ago. 那個送餐人已經離開15分鐘。

II. 外賣餐館 Takeout Restaurants

外賣餐館情景對話
Situational Dialogues at Take-out Restaurants

I. 外賣接單 Take-Out Orders

電話接單 Taking Orders on the Phone

情景對話 I　Dialogue I

A=Waitress 女服務員　B=Guest 顧客

A：China House, may I help you?

A：中國城，我能幫你忙嗎？

B：Yes, I would like to order something to be picked.

B：是的，我想訂一些外賣。

A：Sure, go ahead please.

A：當然可以，請講。

B：I would like to have three chicken broccoli lunches with two wonton soups and one egg drop soup.

B：我想要三份芥蘭雞午餐，兩份餛飩湯，和一份蛋花湯。

A: Anything else?　　A：還要別的嗎？

B: That's it.　　B：就這些了，

A: What's your Phone number please?　請問你的電話號碼是多少？

B: 646-688-5622. And when will it be ready?

B: 646-688-5622．多長時間可以做好？

A: In about 15 minutes.　　　A：大概十五分鐘。

B: Ok, I'll be there shortly.　　B：好的，我馬上到那裏。

A: Thank you for calling, see you later.　A：謝謝你打電話來。待會見。

B: You're welcome, bye.　　B：不用謝了，再見。

情景對話 II Dialogue II

A=Waitress 女服務員 B=Guest 顧客

A: Chinese Food King, how can I help you?　A：食王，我可以幫你忙嗎？

B: Yes，I'd like to order something to go.　B：是的，我想訂一些外賣菜。

A: Thank you. Go ahead please.　A：謝謝，請講。

B: One Egg Roll.　B：一份春卷。

A: Uh-huh.　A：可以。

B: Two pints of Wonton Soup.　B：兩品脫餛飩湯。

A: Uh-huh，two pints of Wonton Soup.　A：可以，兩品脫餛飩湯。

B: One quart of Beef & Broccoli.　B：一誇脫牛肉炒芥蘭菜。

A: Yes，one quart of Beef & Broccoli.

A：可以，一誇脫牛肉炒芥蘭菜。

B: One order Subgum Wonton.　B：一份什錦餛飩。

A: OK, one order Subgum Wonton.　A：可以，一份什錦餛飩。

B: And three orders Happy Family.　B：三份全家福。

A: Three orders Happy Family. I got that.　A：三份全家福，明白了。

B: Can you make one Happy Family extra hot, one mild, and one just regular hot?　B：你可以把一份全家福做成特別辣，一份一點辣，還有一份祇要一般辣。

A: No problem.　A：沒問題。　　B: That'll do it.　B：就這些了。

A: May I have your phone number, please?　A：請問你的電話號碼？

B: 888-862-1018 and extension 123 and how long will it take?

B：888-862-1018,分機號碼是123。要多長時間？

A: About 15 minutes, is that Ok?　A：大概15分鐘，可以嗎？

B: Great, thank you very much, bye.　B：可以，謝謝，再見。

A: You're welcome, bye!　A：不用謝，再見！

II. 外賣餐館 Takeout Restaurants

情景對話 III　Dialogue III

A=Waiter 服務員　B=Guest 顧客

A: New Star's，May I help you?　A：新星，我能幫你忙嗎？

B: Yes，I'd like to order some food to take out.

B：是的，我想訂一些外賣。

A: Sure, go ahead please.　A：當然可以，請講。

B：One order Chicken Wings with French Fries, please.

B：一份鷄翅膀加炸薯條。

A：Oh，I see，but we don't have it, sorry about that.

A：哦，我知道了，但是我們沒有，很抱歉。

B：Forget it．I would like a fried Wonton instead.

B：算了，我要一份炸餛飩代替。

A: Thank you．What else?　A：謝謝，還要什麽？

B：Two orders Steak Kew．　B：兩份"上的球"。

A: Excuse me?　A：對不起(請再講一遍)。

B: Steak Kew!!　B："士的球"！

A: Where is it on the menu?　A：它在菜單上哪裏？

B: It's under Chef's Special menu．　B：在厨師特別菜部份。

A: I'm sorry, I'm new here．Could you tell me the number please?

A：對不起，我是新來的，你能告訴我它的號碼嗎？

B: It's C 20, you got that?　B：C 20，你找到了嗎？

A: Oh, I got it．　A：噢，我找到了。

B: One more thing，could you make chicken Steak Kew with white sauce instead of brown sauce?

B：還有一件事，你能把芥蘭鷄的黑醬汁換成白醬汁嗎？

A: Of course．　A：當然可以。

B: Great, let me have three pints of that.　B：太好了，我要三品脱。

A: Anything else?　A：還有別的嗎？

B: No, that's it.　B：不，沒有了。

A: Let me repeat your order to make sure it's correct.

A：讓我重復一遍來核對一下是否正確。

B: Good.　B：好的。

A: One fried wonton…　A：一份炸餛飩……

情景對話 IV　Dialogue IV

A=Waiter 服務員　B=Guest 顧客

A: China King, May I help you?　A：皇家，我能幫你忙嗎？

B: Yes, I want to place an order.　B：是的，我要訂菜。

A: Great, go ahead please.　A：好的，請講吧。

B: May I ask you a question first?　B：我可以先問你一個問題嗎？

A: Sure.　A：當然可以。

B: What's in the Bao Bao Platter?　B：寶寶盤有什麼？

A: There are five kinds of appetizers all together. And it's two of each, they are Egg rolls, Beef on Stick, Shrimp Toast, Fantail shrimps, and Pork Dumplings.　A：它們有五種開胃食物，面且每樣都有二個，它們是春卷、牛肉串、蝦吐士、鳳尾蝦和豬肉餃。

B: Oh, I see. It sounds good. Let me have that and two No.3 Combination Dinner please.

B：噢，我懂了，聽起來挺好的，我要那個寶寶盤還有兩份三號晚餐。

A: Anything else?　A：還有嗎？

B: That's everything. I'll pick it up at ten after eight.

B：就這些了，我8點10分來拿。

61

II. 外賣餐館　Takeout Restaurants

A: No problem. Phone number please?　A：沒問題。請問你的電話是？

B: 646-688-5622.　B：646-688-5622。

A: Thank you.　A：謝謝。

B: When will it be ready?　B：何時可以做好？

A: In ten minutes.　A：十分鐘。

B: Thank you, bye.　B：謝謝，再見。

A: You're welcome, bye.　A：不用謝，再見。

情景對話 V　Dialogue V

A=Waiter 服務員　B=Guest 顧客

A: Dragon City, can I help you?　A：龍城，我能幫你嗎？

B: Yes! I'm calling from Downtown hospital.
B：是的！我是從下城醫院打來的…

A: Is that Tony?　A：是湯尼嗎？　B: Yes.　B：是的。

A: This is Kim. How are you, Tony?　A：我是肯恩，你好嗎，湯利？

B: Good. How are you, Kim?　B：很好，你好嗎，肯恩？

A: Fine. Are you happy on your vacation?　A：很好。渡假愉快嗎？

B: Yes. How is your business going?
B：是的，很愉快。你的生意怎麼樣？

A: Great.　A：很好。

B: Well, let me have two Sweet and Sour chicken, one with sauce on the side, the other one with the sauce together with chicken, and...
B：這樣，我要兩個甜酸雞，一個帶調味汁，分開，一個放在一起，還有……

A: Excuse me. Is it the Lunch Special or regular order (Pint or Quart)?
A：對不起，它是特別午餐選是一般的菜？

B: Oh Sorry, I mean the Lunch Special. B：噢，我是指特別午餐。

A: That's OK. I got it. A：沒關系。我懂了。

B: And one Chicken Broccoli Lunch just steam, no sauce, I won't it pick it up until 7 o'clock.

B：還有一份芥蘭鶏午餐，衹要蒸的，不要醬汁。我七點鐘才來拿菜。

A: OK, see you at 7 o' clock, Tony! A：可以，那麼，七點見。

B: Bye, Kim. B：再見！肯恩。

情景對話 VI Dialogue VI

A=Waiter 服務員 B=Guest 顧客

A: Number One Kitchen, May I help you? A：第一餐館，我可以幫你嗎？

B: Yes, I want to place an order for pick up.

B：是的，我想訂菜，自己來拿。

A: Sure, but, hold on please. A：當然可以，但是，請等一會兒。

A: Thank you for waiting, go ahead please. A：謝謝你等待，請繼續講。

B: One order dumplings and one extra ginger sauce (dumpling sauce)，please. Could you make that 4 pieces steamed and 4 fried? B：一份餃子，另外一份（生姜醬汁），可以做成四個是蒸的；四個是炸的嗎？

A: Well, if you like. A：可以，如果你喜歡的話。

B: Thank you very much, and I need two more things…

B：非常感謝。 我還要兩份…

送餐寫地址實况會話 Delivery Conversations

情景對話 I Dialogue I

W=Waiter 服務員 G=Guest 顧客

W: China Buffet, may I help you? W：中國自助餐我能幫你忙嗎？

G: Do you deliver? G：你們有送餐嗎？

II. 外賣餐館 Takeout Restaurants

W: Sorry we don't.　　　　　　W：對不起，我們沒有送餐。

G: Thank you. Good bye.　G：謝謝，再見。　W: Bye.　W：再見。

情景對話 II Dialogue II

W=Waiter 服務員　G=Guest 顧客

W: Panda, may I help you?　　　W：熊貓，我能幫你忙嗎？

G: Yes, do you deliver?　　　　G：你們有送餐嗎？

W: Yes, we do.　　　　　　　　W：是的，我們有送餐。

G: Great, I want 2 pints Beef Mushroom.

G：太好了，我要兩品脫牛肉蘑菇。

G: That's it.　　　　　　　　G：就這些了。

W: Your phone number and address please.　W：你的電話號碼和地址？

G: Phone number is 973-123-4567 and address is 75 E. Broadway Suite 222.

G：電話是973-123-4567和地址是東百老匯75號222室。

W: Excuse me, how do you spell "Broadway" please?

W：對不起，請問怎樣拼寫"百老匯"？

G: It's B-R-O-A-D-W-A-Y.　G：它是B-R-O-A-D-W-A-Y.

W: Is it "B" or "D"?　W：是"B"還是"D"？

G: It's B as in Boy.　G：是男孩的"Boy"中的"B"。

W: I got it, thank you and it'll be ready in about 15 to 20 minutes.

W：我懂了。大概15到20分鐘可以好。

G: Great, please tell the delivery man to press 222 button in the lobby.

G：很好，請告訴送餐人在大堂，按222鈴。

W: Okay, I'll.　　　　　　　W：可以，我會的。

G: What's the total?　　　　G：總共多少錢？

W: That's $24.50. By the way, our drivers don't carry cash with them. They

only accept exact change.

W: 總共$24.50。W：我們的司機不帶現金。他們祇接受正好的錢。

G: Okay, thank your bye.　　G：謝謝，再見。

W: You're welcome, bye.　　W：不用謝，再見。

情景對話 III Dialogue III

W=Waiter 服務員　G=Guest 顧客

W: Wing King Restaurant, may I help you?

W：鷄翅王餐館，我能幫你忙？

G: How late are you open till?　G：你們開到幾點？

W: Eleven o'clock.　W：11:00點。

G: Good. I want three quarts of Seafood Chow Mein, one quart of House Special Fried Rice, 2 big order Spare Ribs please. That's it.

G: 好，我要三誇脫海鮮炒緬，一誇脫本樓炒飯、二個大份量的排骨，就這些了。

W: Will that be delivered or will you pick it up?

W: 這是送餐還是自己來拿？

G: Deliver please. G：請送餐。

W: Phone and address please?　W：電話和地址？

G: 347-123-4567 and the Sheraton Hotel at Seaport.

G: 電話是347-123-4567。地址是碼頭邊的喜來登酒店。

W: Where is it?　W: 它在哪裏？

G: Well, It is right next to the World Financial Center.

G: 這樣，就在世界金融中心旁邊。

W: I'm sorry, I'm not familiar with the area. Could you please give me the exact address?

65

II. 外賣餐館 Takeout Restaurants

W：對不起，我對這個區不大熟悉，可以給我詳細的地址嗎？

G: Sure. It is 168 Wall Street.　G：當然可以，是華爾街168號。

W: Okay, I got it. What is your Room Number?
W：好的，明白了。您的房間號是多少？

G: I'm afraid that the Security won't let you in. Just give me a call when you are in the lobby and I'll go down and pick it up.　G：恐怕保安人員不會讓您進來。當你到達大堂時給我打電話，我會下去取。

W: Okay, our delivery man will be there in 15 minutes.
W：好！我們15分鐘後會送到那裏。

G: Thank you.　G：謝謝。

W: You're welcome. Thank you for your business, bye-bye.
W：不用謝。謝謝光顧，再見。

II. 櫃枱接單會話 Taking Orders at the Counter

情景對話 I Dialogue I

A=Cashier 收銀員　B=Guest 顧客

A: Hi! How are you?　　　　　A：嗨！你好嗎？

B: Good, how are you?　　　　B：很好，你好嗎？

A: Fine.　　　　　　　　　　A：很好。

B: I want 2 pints Pepper Steak, one quart Beef Chop Suey.
B：我要2品脫青椒牛，1誇脫牛雜碎。

A: That's it?　　　　　　　　A：就這些嗎？

B: Yes.　　　　　　　　　　　B：是的。

A: For here or to go?　　　　A：這裏吃還是外賣？

B: To go please. How long?　　B：外賣的。要多長時間？

A: Ten minutes.　　　　　　　A：十分鐘。

B: Good. I'm going to he next door, and I'll be right back.

B：好，我去隔壁商店就回來。

A: Ok, no problem.　　　　　A：可以，沒問題。

情景對話 II　Dialogue II

A=Cashier 收銀員　B=Guest 顧客

A: Yes, may I help you?　　　A：我能幫你嗎？

B: I'm waiting for my food.　　B：我正在等我的菜。

A: what's your order, sir?　　A：你訂的是什麼菜，先生？

B: General Tsao's Chicken and Shrimp Lobster Sauce.

B：佐宗雞與蝦龍糊。

A: Let me check on it.　　　　A：讓我幫你查一查。

B: Thank you.　　B：謝謝。

A: It's almost ready. Could you wait for another minute, please?

A：它馬上好了，可以再等一會嗎？

B: OK, no problem.　　　　B：可以，沒問題。

情景對話 III　Dialogue III

A=Cashier 收銀員　B=Guest 顧客

A: Hi! How are you?　　　　A：嗨，你好嗎？

B: Fine, how are you?　　　　B：我很好，你好嗎？

A: Very good, may I help you?　A：很好，我能幫你嗎？

B: Yes, let me have one pint of shrimp & broccoli, one quart of beef mushroom, and two cans of Pepsi, please.

B：是的，我要一品脫芥蘭蝦，1誇脫蘑菇牛，2罐百事可樂。

A: Anything else?　　　　A：還要別的嗎？

67

II. 外賣餐館 Takeout Restaurants

B: That's it. How long will it take?　B: 就這些了，要多長時間？

A: About 10 minutes.　A: 大概十分鐘。

B: Great! How much is it?　B: 太好了，多少錢？

A: It's $26.10.　A: 總共＄26.10。

B: Shall I pay now then?　B: 現在付錢嗎？

A: Whatever you like.　A: 隨便。

B: Let me pay now then.　B: 那麼我現在付。

A: That would be fine.　A: 那好。

B: Here's 30 dollars.　B: 這是三十元。

A: Excuse me. Do you have 10 cents change?

A: 對不起，你有一角的零錢嗎？

B: I might have…Yes, I've got that.　B: 我可能有…是的，找到了。

A: Great. It makes it easier for me. Here is your $4 change and receipt. Thank you! And take a seat please while you're waiting.

A: 太棒了，這容易多了。這是找給你的四元和收據，謝謝！你等的時候，請坐一會兒。

B: Thank you.　B: 謝謝你。

A: You're welcome.　A: 不用謝。

情景對話 IV　Dialogue IV

A=Cashier 收銀員　B=Guest 顧客

A: Hi! How are you doing?　A: 嗨，你好嗎？

B: Pretty good, how are you doing?　B: 很好，你好嗎？

A: Very well, what do you want for dinner?　A: 很好，晚餐要什麼？

B: I don't know yet, give me a couple of minutes please.

B: 我還不知道，請給我兩三分鐘。

A: Ok! Take your time, please.　　A：好的，請慢慢來。

A: Are you ready?　　A：你好了嗎？

B: Yes, No.2 combination, one order of Happy Family, extra broccoli, one pint of wonton soup, no scallions.　　B：是的，2號組合套餐，一份全家福，加西蘭花，1品脫餛飩湯，不要葱。

A: I got it. Will that be all?　　A：我清楚了，就這些了嗎？

B: Yes, when will it be ready?　　B：是的，多長時間可以好？

A: About 10 or 15 minutes, here is your number and have a cup of tea while you wait. I'll call you when it's done.

A：大概十至十五分鐘，這是你的號碼。可以先喝一杯茶。好的時候我會叫你。

B: Thank you.　　B：謝謝你。

A: You're welcome.　　A：不用謝。

櫃枱出菜 Serving Food at the Counter

情景對話 I Dialogue I

A=Cashier 收銀員　B=Guest 顧客

A: Phone No.646-688-5622 please!　　A：電話號碼：646-688-5622。

B: Yes, right here.　　B：在這裏。

A: Here you go. What kind of sauce do you want, sir?

A：這是你的訂菜，你要哪種醬汁？

B: 3 bags duck sauce, 2 bags soy sauce pleases, no mustard, and may I have 2 cokes too?

B：三包酸梅醬，兩包醬油，不要芥菜醬，我還可以加兩罐可樂嗎？

A: Sure.　　A：當然可以。

II. 外賣餐館 Takeout Restaurants

B: How much all together?　　B：總共多少錢？

A: That's $20 even.　　A：20元整。

B: Here is 20 Dollars.　　B：這是20塊。

A: Here is your receipt, thank you. And enjoy your Lunch.

A：這是你的收據，謝謝。請享用你的午餐

B: I will. Thank you. Bye.　　B：我會的。謝謝。再見。

A: Bye.　　A：再見。

情景對話 II Dialogue II

A=Cashier 收銀員　B=Guest 顧客

A：Excuse me, sir! Your order is ready.　A：嗨，先生！你的菜好了。

B: Good.　　B：太好了。

A: Here it is. Take some sauce over there on the table.

A：這就是，請在那邊桌子上拿一些醬汁。

B: I'm all set. Thank you.　　B：我這樣就行了，謝謝。

A: You're welcome. That's $16.50. Here is your change, thank you. And hold it like this please.

A：不用謝，它是 $16.50。這是找回給你的零錢，謝謝，請這樣拿。

B: Oh! Thank you.　　B：噢！謝謝。

A: You're welcome. See you next time, bye!　A：不用謝。下次再見。

B: I'll be back soon. Bye!　　B：我很快會再來的，再見。

III. 堂吃酒樓用語
Dine-in Restaurants Expressions

- 中式菜肴 Chinese Dishes
- 餐桌服務式餐館情景對話
  Situational Conversations at Table Service Restaurants
- 預定座位 Making Reservations
- 請賓客入座 Seating the Guests
- 爲賓客點菜 Taking Orders
- 菜式介紹 Dishes Introductions
- 名酒介紹 Wine Introductions
- 用餐服務 Meals Service
- 徵求意見 Asking For Suggestions
- 用餐結賬 Paying the Bills

III. 堂吃酒樓用語
Dine-in Restaurants Expressions

I. 中式菜肴 Chinese Dishes

雞類 Chicken Dishes

Baked Chicken	叫化雞
Braised Chicken with Brown Sauce	紅燒雞
Cashews with Chicken	腰果雞丁
Chicken in Casserole	砂鍋雞
Chicken Slices　炒雞片　　Chicken with Orange Peel	陳皮雞
Crispy Chicken　脆皮雞　　Deep-Fried Chicken	當紅炸子雞
Diced Chicken with Chili and Peanuts	宮保雞丁
Marinated Chicken	醬雞
Pan-Fried Chicken Slices	芙蓉雞片
Smoked Chicken	熏雞
Spiced Chicken	五香雞
Steamed Chicken with Scallion	蔥油雞
Steamed Chicken Wrapped in Lotus Leaves	荷葉蒸雞
Steamed Spring Chicken	清蒸雞
Steamed Chicken with Chili Sauce	口水雞
Tender Boiled Chicken with Soy Sauce	白斬雞

鴨類 Duck Dishes

Crispy Fried Duck	香酥鴨

Duck & Green Soy Bean in Spicy Sauce	毛豆燒鴨
Duck Tongue with Basil	九層塔鴨舌
Marinated Duck	醬鴨
Mushrooms with Duck Feet	白靈菇扣鴨掌
Quan Ju De Roast Duck	全聚德烤鴨
Smoked Tea Duck 樟茶仔鴨	Spicy Duck Tongue 小辣鴨舌
Toasted Duck Rolls with Ham	燒鴨卷
Yam Gelatin Duck	魔芋燒鴨

鵝類 Goose Dishes

Braised Goose Webs with Oyster Sauce	耗油扒鵝掌
Crispy Fried Goose 香酥鵝	Crispy Goose with Plum 梅子脆皮鵝
Crispy Roast Goose 脆皮火鵝	Steamed Cured Goose 蒸臘鵝
Roast Goose 燒鵝	Spicy Goose Wings and Webs 滷鵝掌
Fried Slice Goose in Fruit Sauce 果汁煎鵝脯	

牛肉類 Beef Dishes

Beef Curry 咖喱牛肉	Beef with Beijing Sauce 京醬牛肉
Beef with Broccoli 芥蘭牛肉	Beef with Green Pepper 青椒牛肉
Beef with Hot Pepper 麻辣牛肉	Braised Beef with Potatoes 牛肉炖土豆
Ginger Beef 姜絲牛柳	OX Tripe in Hot Pot 紅燒牛尾
Quick-Fried Beef with Scallion 葱爆牛肉	Simmered Beef 炖牛肉
Steamed Beef Ribs in Black Bean Sauce 豉汁牛仔骨	
Stewed Beef in Clear Soup 清炖牛肉	Stewed Beef 水煮牛肉
Stir-Fried Beef in Oyster Sauce 耗油牛肉	Willow Beef 川味牛柳

III. 堂吃酒樓用語 Dine-in Restaurants Expressions

羊肉類 Mutton Dishes

Crispy Fried Lamb Breast 酥炸羊脯		Fried Mutton	煎羊排
Instant-Boiled Mutton 刷羊肉		Mutton Steak in Red Sauce 羊肉扒	
Mutton with Beijing Scallion 京葱羊肉		Roast Lamb Chops	烤羊排
Sautéed Lamb Slices with Scallion 葱爆羊肉		Roast Mutton	烤羊肉
Roast Lamb Leg 烤羊腿		Stewed Lamb Trotters	扒羊蹄
Stewed Mutton Clear Soup 清炖羊肉		Stewed Spiced Mutton	燒羊肉

猪肉類 Pork Dishes

Braised Dongpo Pork 東坡方肉	Braised Pig Feet in Brown Sauce 醬猪手	
Chicken and Cucumber Salad		凉拌三絲
Crispy-Skinned Roasted Goose		燒鵝
Crispy-Skinned Roasted Pork 燒猪	Fish-flavor Port Shreds	魚香肉絲
Meat Balls Braised with Brown Sauce		四喜丸子
Port Lungs in Chili Sauce 夫妻肺片	Roast Pork	叉燒
Sautéed Preserved Pork with Dried Tofu Slices		臘肉炒香幹
Sautéed Shredded Pork in Sweet Bean Sauce		京醬肉絲
Sautéed Sliced Pork with Pepper and Chili		回鍋肉皮
Sautéed Sliced Pork, Eggs and Black Fungus		木須肉
Shredded Pork with Vegetables, Sichuan Style		川味小炒
Sweet and Sour Spare Ribs		糖酸排骨
Steamed Pork Coasted with Rice Powder		粉蒸肉
Stewed Pork Ball in Brown Sauce		紅燒獅子頭

蔬菜類 Vegetable Dishes

Dry-Fried String Beans	幹煸四季豆
Eggplant with Garlic Sauce	魚香茄子
Fresh Mushrooms with Bamboo Shoots	鮮菇竹笋
Minced Pork with Cellophane Noodle	螞蟻上樹
Potato with Green Pepper	青椒土豆絲
Sautéed Cabbage with Spicy Sour Sauce	醋溜芽白
Sautéed Chinese Cabbage	金鈎白菜
Sautéed Shanghai Cabbage with Dry Pepper	炒小白菜
Sautéed Spinach with Garlic	蒜炒菠菜
Spicy Whole Green Hot Pepper	虎皮牛角椒

海鮮類 Seafood Dishes

Baked Lobster with Sesame Sauce	香汁烤龍蝦
Boiled Fish with Pickled Cabbage and Chili	酸菜魚
Braised Abalone with Brown Sauce	紅燒鮑魚
Braised Fish Maw with Brown Sauce	紅燒魚肚
Crispy Rice with Sea Cucumber	鍋巴海參
Deep-Fried Shrimp Toast	炸蝦吐司
Deep-Fried Shrimp Balls 炸蝦球　　Fish Lip in Casserole	砂鍋魚唇
Sautéed Squid with Celery	中芹鮮魷
Sea Cucumber and Other Two Delicacies	三鮮海參
Sea Cucumbers with Scallion	葱燒海參
Shark's Fin with Chili Sauce	幹燒魚翅
Shark's Fin with Crab Rose	蟹黃魚翅

III. 堂吃酒樓用語 Dine-in Restaurants Expressions

Shrimp with Popped Rice 蝦仁鍋巴	Spicy Stir-Fried Prawns 幹燒明蝦
Steamed Crab 蒸螃蟹	Steamed Live Fish 清蒸魚
Steamed Scallop with Garlic 蒜蓉蒸扇貝	
Stewed Abalone with Oyster Sauce 耗汁鮑魚片	
Stir-Fried Diced Fish 鬆子魚	Stir-Fried Diced Filet 炒魚片
Stuffed Chicken with Shark's Fin 鷄包翅	Sweet and Sour Fish 糖醋魚

湯類 Soup

Fish Head Soup 砂鍋魚頭湯	Fish with Sour Cabbage Soup 酸菜魚湯
Ham and White Gourd Soup 翡翠蝦蓉湯	Hot and Sour Soup 酸辣湯
Pork Liver with Spinach Soup 肝片菠菜湯	
Pork Stomach with Sour Cabbage Soup 酸菜肚片湯	
Shredded Pork with Pickle Soup 榨菜肉絲湯	
Tomato & Egg Soup 蕃茄蛋湯	West Lake Beef Chowder 西湖牛肉羹
Noodles and Rice 粥粉面粉等主食類	Beef Chow Fun 幹炒牛肉河粉
Congee with Roasted Duck	生滾燒鵝粥
Congee with Roasted Beef	生滾牛肉粥
Congee with Fish Fillet 魚片粥	Fishman's Congee 荔灣艇仔粥
Plain Congee 明火白粥	
Pork Chop with Black Pepper Rice Dish 黑椒猪扒飯	
Preserved Egg & Pork Congee	皮蛋瘦肉粥
Roast Pork Lo Mein 叉燒拌面	
Seafood Fried Rice with Curry Flavor 咖喱海鮮炒飯	
Shrimps with Egg Sauce Rice Dish 滑蛋蝦仁炒飯	
Shredded Pork and Pickles Mein Fun Soup 榨菜肉絲湯米粉	

Shrimp Lo Mein	蝦仁拌面	Shrimp Wontons Noodle Soup	鮮蝦雲吞湯面
Shrimp Wontons	鮮蝦混沌	Singapore Chow Mein Fun	星洲炒米粉
Supreme Soy Sauce Pan Fried Noodle 豉汁皇炒面			
Vegetable's Lo Mein 素菜拌面			

小吃，甜品類 Appetizer, Dessert

Apple Fritter	拔絲蘋果	Banana Fritter	拔絲香蕉
Beef Stew	紅燒牛腩	Bird's Nest in Coconut Milk	椰香燕窩羹
Boiled Tofu	滷水豆腐	Pig's Ear	滷水猪耳
Boiled Egg	滷水鷄蛋	Cantonese Stuffed Been Curd	嚷豆腐
Chicken Feet Cold Served	白雲鳳爪	Eight Treasures Ice	八寶冰
Fried Shrimp Balls	炸蝦丸	Fried White Radish Patty	蘿卜糕
Glutinous Rice Sesame Balls	芝麻球	Plum Juice	酸梅汁
Red Bean Cake	紅豆糕	Red Bean with Milk Ice	紅豆牛奶冰
Steamed Bread Rolls	銀絲卷	Stomach Beef	五香牛肚
Taro Cake	芋頭糕	Tofu Pudding	豆腐花
Vegetarian Rolls	素菜春卷		

III. 堂吃酒樓用語 Dine-in Restaurants Expressions

餐桌服務式餐館情景對話
Situational Conversations at Table Service Restaurants

預定座位 Making Reservations

預訂常用句子 Useful Sentences in Handling Reservations

無法滿足客人的預訂要求 Unable to meet Reservation Requests

I'm sorry; our restaurant is fully booked at that time. Would you mind changing your time? Tables will be available at 7:30pm.

對不起，我們餐廳在那個時間段的座位都已經訂滿了。您是否介意更改一下您的時間呢？晚上7:30會有空桌子。

I'm afraid the tables by the windows are fully reserved. I can't guarantee you a table right now. But we'll try our best.

對不起，靠窗的桌子恐怕都已經被預訂了。我們不能保證一定會爲您保留一張靠窗的桌子，但我們會盡力。

I'm sorry. The tables by the window are all occupied.

對不起，靠近窗口的桌子全都有人了。

Sorry, the Lijing Room has already been reserved, shall we reserve another room for you?

對不起，麗晶房已經訂出去了。我們爲您安排另外一間好嗎？

Sorry, we do not have reservation service today, because we have a banquet service tonight.

對不起，因爲承接了宴會服務，我們今天不對外預訂。

Sorry, we do not have reservation for morning tea.

隊不起，早茶不設訂座服務。

Sorry, but there is only one table left that seats six people.

對不起，祇有一張6人桌了。

確認預訂 Confirming Reservations

I would like to confirm my reservation for tomorrow night, please.
我想確認一下明天晚上的訂座。

You reservation is for the Nanhai Room at 6:30 this evening. What else may I help you with?
您今晚6點半預訂了本餐廳的南海房，請問是否有什麼變更？

Is this a new reservation or a confirmation call?
您這個電話是新的預訂，還是確認預訂呢？

Your reservation / table is confirmed. 您的預訂已經得到確認。

I'm afraid that we have no record of a reservation (for that date) in your name. 恐怕我們沒有您（那天）預訂的記錄。

Shall I make a reservation for you now? 我現在為您預訂好嗎？

When did you make the reservation? 您什麼時候預訂的？

In whose name was the reservation made? 這項預訂是用誰的名字訂的？

更改預訂 Changing Reservations

I'd like to change my reservation from 6:30pm to 7:30pm.
我想把預訂從晚上6:30改到7:30。

We'll change the reservation for you. 我們會為您更改預訂的。

I'd like to change / cancel a reservation. 我要更改/取消一項預訂。

對話 I Dialogue I

Waiterss 服務員　Customer 顧客

Waitress: Hello, this is the "Taste Garden".
服務員：你好，這裏是"風味園"。

Customer: Hello. Can I reserve a table for Saturday?
顧客：你好。我可以預訂一張星期六的桌子嗎？

79

III. 堂吃酒樓用語 Dine-in Restaurants Expressions

Waitress: Sure. How many of you are coming and what time would you like your table? 服務員：當然可以。您幾位？什麼時候進餐？

Customer: Six. We'd like the table at 6:30 Saturday evening.
顧客：六位。我們星期六晚上6:30到。

Waitress: Your name, sir? 服務員：您的名字，先生？

Customer: Michael Dell.
顧客：米高戴爾。

Waitress: Mr. Dell, we'll keep the table for you until 6:50. You know it's always busy on the weekend.
服務員：戴爾先生，我們將為您保留餐桌到6:50。您知道周末顧客總是很多的。

Customer: It's all right. Thank you.
顧客：好的。謝謝您。

Waitress: Good-bye. 服務員：再見。

對話 II Dialogue II

R: Reservation Clerk 預訂服務員　G：Guest 顧客

R: Good afternoon! This is Pearl Restaurant. Michael is speaking. May I help you? 預訂服務員：下午好！這是明珠餐館，我是服務員米高。請問有什麼可以幫到您？

G: I'd like to reserve a table for two tonight, please.
顧客：我想今晚預訂一張兩人桌。

R: For what time, sir? 預訂服務：請問訂在什麼時候？

G: Around 7:30.　　顧客：7點30分左右。

R: May I have your name and phone number please, sir?
預訂服務員：可以留下您的姓名和聯繫電話嗎？

G: Jack. And my number is 212-345-6789.

顧客：杰克。我的電話是212-345-6789。

R: Would you please spell it?　預訂服務員：請您拼一下可以嗎？

G: B-A-K-E-R.　　　顧客：B-A-K-E-R.

R: Is that D as in dog or B as in Boy?

預訂服務：是"dog"的"D"還是"Boy"的"B"？

G: B as in boy.　　　顧客："Boy"裏的"B"。

R: Thank you! A table for two at 7:30 this evening for Mr. Baker.

預訂服務員：謝謝！貝克先生，您預訂的是一張今晚7點30分的兩人桌。

G: That's right.　顧客：是的。

R: Thank you for calling, Mr. Baker. By the way, as that is the peak hour, we only can keep your table for half an hour. That means you should come before 8:00. We look forward to welcoming you.

預訂服務員：謝謝您致電本店，貝克先生。順便提醒您，因爲是高峰時段，所以您的預訂我們祇能爲您保留半個小時，請您在8點之前到達。我們期待您的光臨！

無法滿足預訂要求 Unable to meet reservation Request

R: Reservation Clerk 預訂服務員　G：Guest 顧客

G: Hello, is that the Happy Hour Restaurant?

顧客：喂，是快樂時光餐廳嗎？

R: Speaking. May I help you?

預訂服務員：是的。需要幫忙嗎？

G: Yes. I'd like a table for eight at 7:00 this evening. Can you arrange it for us?　顧客：您好！我預訂今晚7點鐘的8人餐臺一張，您們能夠爲我們安排一下嗎？

81

III. 堂吃酒樓用語 Dine-in Restaurants Expressions

R: Just a minute. I'll check if there any availability. (After a while) I'm sorry sir. There isn't any tables left for 7:00, but we can give you one at 8:30. Would you like to make a reservation at that time?

預訂服務員：請稍等，我查查還有沒有空位。（稍過一會兒）。對不起，先生。今晚7點鐘的座位已經訂滿了，但是我們可以安排您8點半的座位。您覺得安排在那個時間可以嗎？

G: Well, let me see. It seems a little late.

顧客：嗯，讓我想想。這似乎晚了些。

R: Usually, the restaurant will be quieter at that time, sir.

預訂服務員：先生，通常那個時間餐廳比較安靜。

G: That's the truth, and we need a quiet place in fact.

顧客：這倒是事實，而且，實際上我們需要一個安靜的地方。

R: Then I will recommend the West Lake Room. It is quiet and spacious. And we offer free fruit juice after 8:30.

預訂服務員：那我推薦您去西湖房，那裏比較安靜，而且寬敞。并且我們會爲8點半以後來就餐的顧客免費送果汁。

G: Fine. I change the time to 8:30.

顧客：好的。那就把時間改在8點半吧。

R: Very good, sir. A table for eight at 8:30 this evening in West Lake Room is confirmed. May I have your name please?

預訂服務員：好的，先生。今晚8點半的一張8人臺，西湖房。請問貴姓？

G: It's Smith.

顧客：史密斯。

R: Thank you very much, Mr. Smith. Bye.

預訂服務員：非常感謝，史密斯先生。再見。

迎接賓客 Greeting Guests

對話1 Dialogue1

Waitress: Good evening. Welcome! Do you have a reservation?

女服務員：晚上好，歡迎光臨！請問您預訂了嗎？

Customer: No, I'm afraid we don't.　顧客：沒有。

Waitress: How many are there in your party?

女服務員：請問您們共有多少人？

Customer: Eight.　　顧客：8個。

Waitress: I'm sorry, we don't have a table for eight people now, but there will be one after about 15 minutes, do you mind waiting in the lounge? You can have a drink there or reading newspaper.

女服務員： 非常抱歉，現在沒有能坐8個人的餐桌，要等大概20分鐘後才有。您們願意到休息室等等嗎？ 您們可以在那裏喝些飲料，也可以看看報紙。

Customer: That's a good idea.　　顧客：這是個好主意。

Waitress: May I have your name?　女服務員：我能記下您的名字嗎？

Customer: Gilbert.　　　　　　顧客：吉爾伯特。

Waitress: We'll seat you when we have a table.

女服務員：一有位置我們就會爲您安排的。

對話 II Dialogue II

Waitress: Excuse me, sir. We can seat your party now.

女服務員：先生，您好！現在有位置了。

Customer: Good.

顧客：好的。

Waitress: Please step this way.

女服務員：請往這邊走。

83

III. 堂吃酒樓用語 Dine-in Restaurants Expressions

對話2 Dialogue 2

Waitress: Good afternoon, sir.　服務員：下午好，先生。

Customer: Good afternoon. Do you have a table for three?

顧客：下午好。有3個人用餐的空桌嗎？

Waitress: Yes, sir. How about the table near the window?

服務員：有的，先生。靠窗那張桌子可以嗎？

Customer: That would be nice. Thanks.　顧客：很好。謝謝。

Waitress: Come with me, please.　服務員：請跟我來。

對話3 Dialogue3

Waitress: Good evening. Welcome to our restaurant. Your table is over there. Would you please come this way?　服務員：晚上好。歡迎光臨我們的飯店。您的桌子在那邊。請走這邊。

Customer: Thank you.　顧客：謝謝。

Waitress: Take a seat please. Here is the menu. I'll come back in just a moment to take your order.

服務員：請坐。這是菜單。我過會兒再來幫您點菜。

Customer: Thank you.　顧客：謝謝。

對話4 Dialogue4

Waitress: Good evening, sir.　服務員：晚上好，先生。

Customer: Gee! So busy in here! Could you find me a table for one, please?

顧客：呀！這麼多人！能給我安排一張一個人的餐桌嗎？

Waitress: Have you reserved a table?　服務員：您預訂了餐桌了嗎？

Customer: No, I haven't.　顧客：不，我沒有。

Waitress: Well I'm sorry , but I don't think I can help you at the moment. We're filled up right now.

服務員：那對不起了，我現在也沒辦法。這會兒擠滿了。

Customer: But I'm leaving this city tomorrow. I'm told the food served here is excellent. I do not want to leave this city with regret.

顾客：可我明天就离开这里了。我听说这里的菜烧得特别好。我不想带着遗憾离开这。

Waitress: Surely you won't. But do you mind waiting or sharing a table?

服务员：不，当然不会。可是您介意等一会儿，或者和别人同桌吗？

Customer: It doesn't matter.

顾客：都没有关系。

Waitress: All right. Would you please wait in the lounge? I'll inform you when there's a table available.

服务员：好的。请到休息室等好吗？有空桌了我再告诉您。

Customer: Thanks.

顾客：谢谢。

请宾客入座 Seating the Guests

Hostess: Good evening, sir.

女迎宾：先生，晚上好。

Guest: Good evening. Could you find me a table for one, please?

客人：晚上好。请给我安排一张一人桌，好吗？

Hostess: I'm afraid all our tables are taken, sir. Could you wait until a table is free, please?

女迎宾：我恐怕所有的位子都坐满了，先生。请排队等到有空位好吗？

Guest: Well, how long will it take?

客人：好的，要等多久呢？

Hostess: About fifteen minutes, sir.

女迎宾：大约15分钟，先生。

Guest: That's a bit too long.

客人：这可有点太久了。

Hostess: Would you mind sharing a table, then?

女迎宾：那么您是否愿意与别人同桌？

III. 堂吃酒樓用語 Dine-in Restaurants Expressions

Guest: Well, I'd rather wait. 客人：那我寧可等一下。

Hostess: Could you take a seat over there and I'll inform you when a table is free. 女迎賓：請那邊坐。有了空桌我就告訴你。

Guest: That's fine. 客人：好。

（Fifteen minutes later when a table is free.）(15分鐘後，當有空桌時)

Hostess: We have a table for you sir this way, please. We are very sorry for the delay. 女迎賓：現在有空桌了，先生。請這邊走。非常抱歉耽擱了您的時間。

為賓客點菜 Taking Orders

對話1 Dialogue1

Waitress: May I take your order, sir? 服務員：您現在點菜嗎，先生？

Customer: I haven't seen a menu yet. May I have one?
顧客：我還沒看到菜單呢？可以給我一份菜單嗎？

Waitress: I'm so sorry. I thought the waitress who seated you had given you a menu. Here's one, sir.
服務員：非常抱歉。我還以為剛才給您引坐的服務員已經把菜單給您看過了。請看菜單，先生。

Customer: Thank you.
顧客：謝謝。

對話 2 Dialogue 2

Waitress: What will you have, sir? 服務員：您吃點什麼，先生？

Customer: Can I have a set lunch? 顧客：我可以要一套午餐嗎？

Waitress: Which one? 服務員：要哪一種？

Customer: Fish, Cucumber Salad and Egg Drop Soup.
顧客：魚，黃瓜色拉和蛋花湯。

Waitress: Anything to drink?　　　服務員：要飲料嗎？

Customer: Yes, a Heineken.　　　顧客：是的，一瓶喜力啤酒。

Waitress: Good, a set lunch and a Heineken. I'll bring them right away.

服務員：好的。一套午餐和一瓶喜力啤酒。馬上就送來。

對話3 Dialogue 3

Waitress: Have you decided on something, sir?

服務員：請問你決定點什麼菜了嗎，先生？

Customer: Yes. I'll take Apple Juice, Tomato and Egg Soup and Sichuan Ginger Beef.

顧客：是的。我要果汁，西紅柿鷄蛋湯和四川牛柳。

Waitress: That's OK. One Tomato and Egg Soup, one Apple Juice, one Sichuan Ginger Beef. Anything else?　服務員：好的。一份西紅柿鷄蛋湯，一杯果汁，一份四川牛柳。還有什麼嗎？

Customer: No, thank you.　　　顧客：不要了，謝謝。

Waitress: How about coffee?　　服務員：咖啡怎樣？

Customer: Yes, why not?　　　顧客：好的，爲什麼不呢？

Waitress: Thank you sir.　　　服務員：謝謝，先生。

對話 4 Dialogue 4

Waitress: Excuse me, sir. Are you ready to order?

服務員：打擾了，先生。請問您現在點菜嗎？

Customer: Yes. I'll take the Cold Duck Webs, Winter Melon Soup and Sichuan Dice Chicken with Chili and Pepper.

顧客：是的。我要拌鴨掌，冬瓜湯和宮保鷄丁。

Waitress: Yes, sir. Do you wish to have anything else?

服務員：好的，先生。還要別的嗎？

87

III. 堂吃酒樓用語 Dine-in Restaurants Expressions

Customer: Mm. Is there any particular dish you would recommend?
顧客：嗯。有什麼特別值得推薦的菜嗎？

Waitress: The Crispy Fish is wonderful tonight. The fish are very fresh. We also have several good sea food dishes, if you like sea food.
服務員：今晚的脆皮魚特別好。魚都很新鮮的。我們還有幾種上好的海鮮菜，如果您喜歡海鮮的話。

Customer: I don't care much for sea food. I think I'll try the Crispy Fish.
顧客：我不太喜歡海鮮。就試試脆皮魚吧。

Waitress: Would you like anything to drink?　服務員：您要點喝的嗎？

Customer: Yes, a bottle of beer. By the way, go easy on chili and garlic. I was told Sichuan food is very hot.　顧客：是的，一瓶啤酒。順便提一下，別放太多辣椒和大蒜。我聽說四川菜很辣。

Waitress: Yes, sir. I'll bring the dishes straight away.
服務員：好的，先生。菜馬上就送來。

菜式介紹 Dish Introductions
對話1 Dialogue1

Waitress: Are you ready to order, sir?

服務員：您現在點菜嗎，先生？

Customer: Yes, but there're so many dishes listed on the menu. It's hard to decide. 顧客：是的，可是菜單上菜式那麼多。真不知道該要哪種。

Waitress: We serve both the regular dishes and the set dinners.

服務員：我們有點菜，也有套餐。

Customer: What does the set dinner include? 顧客：套餐都包括什麼內容？

Waitress: It includes soup, rice, meat, vegetable and tea.

服務員：套餐包括湯，米飯，肉，蔬菜和茶。

Customer: If I order from regular dish, I have more choices. Am I right?

顧客：如果我要點菜，選擇會更多些吧，對嗎？

Waitress: Certainly. You may order anything you like.

服務員：當然。您可以點您喜歡的菜。

對話 2 Dialogue 2

Customer: Waiter! 顧客：服務員！

Waitress: I'll be with you in a moment, sir. 服務員：馬上就來，先生。

Customer: I'd like to try different Chinese dishes. Could you tell me what is good tonight?

顧客：今晚我想品嘗不同的中國菜。你能告訴我今晚有什麼好菜嗎？

Waitress: Oh, yes. We serve different styles of Chinese food, including Cantonese style, Beijing style, and Sichuan style in particular.

服務員：哦，是的。我們供應不同風格的中國菜，包括廣東菜和北京菜，當然還有四川菜更是拿手好戲。

Customer: What different features do they have?

顧客：這些菜都有什麼不同的特點？

Waitress: Generally speaking, Cantonese food is light and clear while Sichuan food has a strong and hot taste. As for Beijing food, it's usually salty and spicy.

服務員：一般來說，廣東菜比較清淡，而四川菜味重而辣。至于北京菜嘛，則比較咸，香料放得多。

Customer: I think I'd like to try some Sichuan food. But don't make it too hot. 顧客：我就試試四川菜吧。可別弄得太辣。

Waitress: All right!

服務員：好的！

III. 堂吃酒樓用語 Dine-in Restaurants Expressions

對話 3 Dialogue 3

Customer: Could I see the menu?　　顧客：能看看菜單嗎？

Waitress: Certainly. Here's the bill of fare.

服務員：當然可以。這是菜單。

Customer: I'd like some Sichuan food. Are there any dishes you would recommend?　　顧客：我想吃四川菜。有什麼好菜你可以推薦嗎？

Waitress: If you like a strong and hot taste, you can try the Fish-Flavored Pork Shreds and Chicken Cubes with Chili.

服務員：如果你喜歡味重而不怕辣的話，你可以嘗嘗魚香肉絲和辣子雞丁。

Customer: It sounds good. Then, give me the works, please. I heard Sliced Chicken with Egg White is your specialty, isn't it?　　顧客：聽起來不錯。就照你說的辦吧。我聽說這裏的芙蓉雞片很有名，是嗎？

Waitress: Oh, yes. It looks tender like bean curd, yet is as delicious as chicken.　　服務員：哦，是的。這道菜看上去跟豆腐一樣嫩，吃起來却像雞肉一樣鮮。

Customer: Do you have any distinguished Chinese spirits?

顧客：你們有什麼中國名酒？

Waitress: Yes, we have Maotai. It's a real Chinese specialty. It's rather strong but won't go to your head.　　服務員：是的，我們有茅臺。這是真正的中國特産。酒勁很大却不上頭。

Customer: Good. I'll take it.

顧客：好。我就要這個。

Waitress: Straight away, sir.

服務員：馬上送來，先生。

對話 4 Dialogue 4

Waitress: Have you decided on anything, sir?

服務員：您決定點什麼菜了嗎，先生？

Customer: Not yet. I don't know much about Chinese food. Could you make some recommendations?

顧客：還沒想好。我對中國菜不大熟悉。你能推薦幾樣菜嗎？

Waitress: The beef is very good tonight. We also have several good chicken dishes, if you like chicken. We have Roast Chicken, Multi-Flavor Chicken, Chicken Cutlets, Chicken in Casserole and so on.

服務員：今晚的牛肉很好。如果您喜歡吃雞的話，我們也有幾款不錯的雞肉菜式。我們有燒雞，怪味雞，白斬雞，砂鍋雞等等。

Customer: I'm not very fond of chicken.

顧客：我不太喜歡雞。

Waitress: What about fish? Fish is one of the specialties of the house. We have Steamed Carp, Sweet and Sour Croaker, Stewed Turtle, Stir-Fried Eel with Brown Sauce.

服務員：魚怎麼樣？魚是本店的名特菜之一。我們有清蒸鯉魚，糖醋黃花魚，清炖甲魚，幹燒黃鱔等。

Customer: I think I'll try the Stewed Turtle.

顧客：那我就嘗嘗清炖甲魚吧。

Waitress: That's a good choice! It's both delicious and nutritious.

服務員：真是好眼力！這道菜既美味可口，又營養豐富。

對話 5 Dialogue 5

Waitress: How did you find the food, sir?

服務員：您覺得這菜怎樣，先生？

III. 堂吃酒樓用語 Dine-in Restaurants Expressions

Customer: Very nice. I've never had any food as delicious as this.

顧客：好極了。我從沒有吃過這麼鮮美的菜肴。

Waitress: I'm glad you've enjoyed it. Do you want anything else?

服務員：很高興您喜歡這裏的菜。您還有別的什麼嗎？

Customer: Do you have anything for dessert?

顧客：你們的甜品有些什麼？

Waitress: Sorry, we don't have much dessert in Chinese restaurants. But we have sweet fruit, if you like. The Lotus Seed Soup is very nice tonight. Would you like to try a bit?

服務員：對不起，中式餐館裏没有太多的的甜點。但如果您喜歡的話，我們有香甜的水果。今晚的蓮子湯特別好。要嘗一嘗嗎？

Customer: Yes, I'll take the Lotus Seed Soup and some pineapple. Thanks.

顧客：好的，那我就來一點蓮子湯和菠蘿吧。謝謝。

Waitress: Straight away, sir.　　服務員：馬上送來，先生。

對話 6 Dialogue 6

Waitress: Would you like to see the menu, sir? The a la carte dishes are on the left side, and the set meals are on the right.

服務員：要看菜單嗎，先生？點菜在左頁面，套餐在右頁。

Customer: Thank you. But Sichuan food, I'm told, is very hot. I don't care, but my children are not fond of hot food. Could you recommend some dishes without chili?

顧客：謝謝。我聽說四川菜都很辣。我倒不在乎，可我的孩子不喜歡辣的食品。你能推薦幾種不辣的菜嗎？

Waitress: Yes, sir. Sichuan food is not always hot in fact. Apart from hot food, we have sweet and sour food, light tasting food, spicy food, multi-flavored food. Which do you prefer?

服務員：好的，先生。川菜并不是都是辣的。除了辣味菜以外，我們還有糖醋味，清香味，五香味，怪味菜等等。您喜歡哪一種？

Customer: I think I'll try the sweet and sour food and the light tasting food.
顧客：我看就試試糖醋味和清香味吧。

Waitress: All right. How about the Sweet and Sour Spare Ribs and Steamed Carp?
服務員：好的，糖醋排骨和清蒸鯉魚怎樣？

Customer: That sounds OK. I'll take them, thanks.
顧客：聽起來不錯。就要這兩種吧，謝謝。

Waitress: With pleasure.
服務員：樂意效勞。

名酒介紹 Wine Introductions

餐前開胃酒 Aperitif

Sommelier: Good evening, sir. Would you care for the aperitif before your meal?
斟酒服務員：晚上好，先生。進餐前要不要來點開胃酒？

Guest: Yes, I think I will. But what would you recommend?
客人：是的，我要。你有什麼可推薦的嗎？

Sommelier: How about a Dry Vermouth or a Sandeman Dry Sherry?
斟酒服務員：來杯不甜的苦艾酒或是聖地曼雪莉酒如何？

Guest: I'm afraid neither are to my taste.
客人：恐怕這兩種都不合我的口味。

Sommelier: Then I recommend the Sweet Vermouth and Dubonnet.
斟酒服務員：那麼我推薦甜的苦艾酒和杜邦內葡萄酒。

III. 堂吃酒樓用語 Dine-in Restaurants Expressions

Guest: The Sweet Vermouth sounds delicious. I'll try that.

客人：甜的苦艾酒聽起來很棒，我想嘗嘗看。

Sommelier: Certainly, sir. A Sweet Vermouth. Just a moment, please.

斟酒服務員：好的，先生。一杯甜苦艾酒。請稍候。

佐餐酒 Table Wine

Sommelier: Good afternoon, sir. Would you like to order some wine with your meal?

斟酒服務員：下午好，先生。您要不要叫點酒來下菜？

Guest: Yes.　客人：好的。

Sommelier: Here is the wine list, sir.　斟酒服務員：請看酒單，先生。

Guest: Thank you. But to be frank, I don't know much about wine. Could you make some recommendations?

客人：謝謝。不過說實話，我對酒不大了解。你能否推薦幾種呢？

Sommelier: I think that a Burgundy or a Bordeaux would go very well with your chicken.　斟酒服務員：我認為勃艮第紅葡萄酒或波爾多紅葡萄酒和您點的雞肉會很相配。

Guest: Fine, I'll try the Burgundy. Then what do you think would go well with our fish?　客人：好，我就嘗嘗勃艮第紅葡萄酒吧。那麼你認為什麼酒配我們點的魚呢？

Sommelier: I would recommend the Chablis. I think this wine would be perfect with your fish.　斟酒服務員：我建議您點夏布麗白葡萄酒。我認為這種酒很適合您點的魚。

Guest: That sounds good. I'll take a half bottle of the Burgundy and a half bottle of the Chablis.　客人：聽起來不錯。我就要半瓶勃艮第紅葡萄酒，半瓶夏布麗白葡萄酒。

Sommelier: Certainly, sir. I'll bring them straight away.

斟酒服務員：好的，先生。馬上就來。

餐後酒 Dessert Wine

Sommelier: Did you enjoy your meal, sir?

斟酒服務員：您吃得愉快嗎，先生？

Guest: Yes, it's great. The chicken was just to my taste and the wine was excellent. 客人：是的，非常好。雞肉正合我的口味，酒也很棒。

Sommelier: Thank you, sir. Would you like a liqueur to complete your meal? 斟酒服務員：謝謝，先生。您要不要來點利口酒？

Guest: Yes, an anisette for my friend and a brandy for myself.

客人：好的，請給我朋友來一杯茴香酒，給我一杯白蘭地。

Sommelier: Certainly, sir. Which brandy would you prefer?

斟酒服務員：好的，先生。請問您要什麼牌子的？

Guest: I'd like an Armagnac, please. 客人：我想要一杯阿爾馬涅克。

Sommelier: Of course, sir. Just a moment, please.

斟酒服務員：好的，先生。請稍候。

斟酒服務 Serving Wine

Sommelier: Your Burgundy, sir. May I serve it now?

斟酒服務員：您點的勃艮第紅葡萄酒，先生。現在可以斟酒了嗎？

Guest: Yes, please. 客人：好的。

Sommelier: (Pours wine) How is it, sir?

斟酒服務員：（斟酒）香味如何，先生？

Guest: Excellent! 客人：太棒了！

Sommelier: May I decant it now to allow it to breathe?

斟酒服務員：我要慢慢倒，好讓香味散發出來嗎？

III. 堂吃酒樓用語 Dine-in Restaurants Expressions

Guest: Yes, go ahead.　客人：好的，請便。

Sommelier: Thank you, sir. Please enjoy your meal.

斟酒服務員：謝謝，先生。請慢用。

用餐服務 Meals Service

對話 1 Dialogue 1

Waitress: Here is the Multi-Flavor Chicken and the Sweet and Sour Croaker, sir.　服務員：這是怪味雞和糖醋黃花魚，先生。

Customer: Mm. It looks nice and smells nice, too.

顧客：嗯。看上去不錯，聞起來也挺香。

Waitress: Would you like to have your soup right now or later?

服務員：您要的湯是現在上還是待會兒上？

Customer: Bring it right now, please. I prefer to have some soup before the main dishes.　顧客：現在上吧。我喜歡先喝點兒湯，再吃主菜。

Waitress: Yes, sir. I'll bring it right away.

服務員：好的，先生。我馬上送來。

對話 2 Dialogue 2

Waitress: Here is your Bean Curd Soup, sir.

服務員：您的豆腐湯來了，先生。

Customer: Bean Curd Soup? But I think I ordered the Onion Soup.

顧客：豆腐湯？我要的是洋蔥湯。

Waitress: Oh! I'm awfully sorry. There must have been some mistake. I'll bring your Onion Soup right away. Just a moment, sir.

服務員：噢！非常抱歉。這裏肯定出了錯。您點的洋蔥湯我馬上就送來。請稍候，先生。

Waitress: Here is the Onion Soup, sir. Pardon me for having kept you waiting so long.

服務員：這是洋葱湯，先生。抱歉讓您久等了。

Customer: It's all right.　　　　顧客：沒關系。

對話 3 Dialogue 3

Waitress: Here comes the Fried Prawns with Tomato Sauce. It's one of the specialties of the house.

服務員：這道菜叫西紅柿汁炸大蝦。這是我們餐館的名特佳肴之一。

Customer: It looks good.

顧客：看上去不錯。

Waitress: This is the Fish-Flavor Pork Shreds. It's the typical Sichuan style.

服務員：這是魚香肉絲。這個是典型的四川菜。

Customer: Is it cooked with fish?

顧客：是和魚一起烹制的嗎？

Waitress: No. It has nothing to do with fish, but it cooked with special condiments, and thus tastes like fish.

服務員：不。和魚没關系，祇是用特殊的調料，結果就有了魚香味。

Customer: It sounds like magic.

顧客：聽起來簡直就像魔術一樣。

Waitress: Here is the Chicken and Mushroom Soup. Very tasty. That's all of your dishes. If you want anything else, just call me, please. Enjoy your meal.

服務員：這是蘑菇鷄湯。非常美味。您的菜上齊了。如果您還需要什麼，請叫我。祝您用餐愉快。

Customer: OK, thank you.

顧客：好的，謝謝。

III. 堂吃酒樓用語 Dine-in Restaurants Expressions

徵求意見 Asking for Suggestions
對話1 Dialogue1

Waitress: Does the food appeal to your appetite, sir?

服務員：這些菜合您的口味嗎？

Customer: Yes, it certainly does. I like it very much.

顧客：很合我的口味。我很喜歡。

Waitress: What do you think of the wine?

服務員：您覺得酒怎樣？

Customer: It's good, too. But I'm afraid it's a bit too strong for my wife.

顧客：酒也不錯。祇是對我太太來說恐怕太烈了點。

Waitress: I'm sorry. I should have recommended some other drink.

服務員：真抱歉。我應該向您推薦別的酒。

Customer: Never mind. It's not your fault. My wife just wanted to try a little. It's a famous and popular wine in China, isn't it? 顧客：沒關係。我太太也很想嘗嘗這種酒。這是中國的名酒吧，是嗎？

Waitress: Yes, it's well-known and popular all over the country. Do you have any criticism of our service or dishes? We'd be grateful if you kindly point out our shortcomings.

服務員：是的。它很有名氣，在我國廣受歡迎。您對我們的服務和食物有什麼意見嗎？如果您能指出我們的不足之處，我們將不勝感激。

Customer: No. Everything is good. We had a nice evening here.

顧客：沒有。一切都很好。今天晚上我們過得很愉快。

Waitress: Thanks for you compliments. Good-bye.

服務員：謝謝您的贊揚。再見。

Customer: Good-bye.

顧客：再見。

對話 2 Dialogue 2

Waitress: How did you like the chicken, sir? It's a specialty of the restaurant.

服務員：您喜歡這個雞肉嗎，先生？這是我們餐廳的風味菜。

Customer: The taste is marvelous, but I didn't expect it would be so hot.

顧客：味道不錯，但是我想不到會這麼辣。

Waitress: I'm sorry. I should have asked if you care for hot food.

服務員：真抱歉。我該事先問一下你是否喜歡辣味菜。

Customer: Never mind. I prefer to take it as it is. Otherwise, it wouldn't have been so typical of Sichuan style. 顧客：不要緊。我倒寧願保留它的原味。否則，那就不是正宗的川菜了。

Waitress: How about the fish? 服務員：這魚怎麼樣？

Customer: It's wonderful. It's the most delicious of all dishes.

顧客：好極了。這是最可口的一道菜了。

Waitress: I'm glad you enjoyed it. But do you mean the other dishes are not as good? 服務員：很高興您喜歡。不過，您是不是說其它菜沒有這麼好？

Customer: No, I didn't mean that. I just mean the fish was the best.

顧客：不，我不是這個意思。我祇是說這道魚是最好的。

Waitress: Would you kindly point out our weaknesses?

服務員：請您指出我們的缺點好嗎？

Customer: Well, sometimes I had to wait too long for dishes, and occasionally, there were one or two pieces of tablewares that didn't look so clean. 顧客：哦，我覺得有時候等菜的時間太長，偶爾一兩件餐具不是很幹净。

Waitress: Thanks for pointing out our weaknesses. We'll do our best to improve our service. 服務員：謝謝您指出我們的缺點。我們一定會盡力改進我們的服務。

III. 堂吃酒樓用語 Dine-in Restaurants Expressions

對話 3 Dialogue 3

Waitress: Do you like the food here, sir?

服務員：您喜歡這裏的菜嗎，先生？

Customer: Yes, I certainly do. 顧客：是的，當然喜歡。

Waitress: Which do you think is the best? 服務員：哪一道菜您認爲最好？

Customer: Well, I have to say all the dishes were very delicious. But I like the shark's fin most.

顧客：嗯，我覺得所有的菜都很美味可口。不過我倒是最喜歡魚翅。

Waitress: Thank you for your compliment. But we sincerely welcome you to point out our shortcomings.

服務員：謝謝您的誇獎。不過我們也真誠地歡迎您指出我們的缺點。

Customer: Well, I personally like to eat in a quiet place. But I found it was a bit noisy here. Besides, I saw some customers smoking in spite of the warning of "No Smoking" on the wall. I would appreciate it if you could stop them. 顧客：我吃飯時喜歡安静。我覺得這裏有些過于嘈雜。另外，我看到有些顧客在吸烟，雖然墙上挂着"禁止吸烟"的牌子。如果你們能阻止他們，我會很高興。

Waitress: Thank you. I'll speak to our manager about it. And I'm sure you'll find the situation much improved when you come next time.

服務員：謝謝。我會把您的意見轉告經理。我相信，下次您再來的時候，會發現已經大大改進了。

用餐結賬 Paying the Bill

在桌面付款 Paying the Bill on the Table

Guest: May I have the bill, please? 客人：請把賬單拿來好嗎？

Waiter: Sure. Here it is. 服務員：好的。給您賬單。

Guest: Thanks. 客人：謝謝。

Waiter: Your bill comes to $65.　　服務員：總共是65元。

Guest: Do you accept credit cards?　　客人：可以刷卡嗎？

Waiter: No sir, cash only.　　服務員：不，先生，祇限現金。

Guest: Here is $70. Keep the change.　　客人：這是70元。不用找零了。

Waiter: It's very kind of you, sir. A 10% service change has already been added to your bill.

服務員：您真客氣，先生。您賬單上已經包括了10%的服務費。

Guest: Oh, I see.　　客人：哦，我明白了。

Waiter: Thank you, sir. We look forward to serving you again.

服務員：謝謝您，先生。歡迎再次光臨。

在收銀處付款 Paying the Bill at the Counter

Cashier: Good afternoon, sir. May I help you?

收銀員：下午好，先生。需要幫忙嗎？

Guest: Yes, I'd like to settle my bill, please. How much is it?

客人：是的，我要買單。一共多少錢？

Cashier: Thank you, sir. Your bill comes to $85.

收銀員：謝謝，先生。一共是85元。

Guest: Here you are.　　客人：給你。

Cashier: Thank you, sir. Have a nice afternoon.

收銀員：謝謝，先生。祝您下午愉快。

用餐券付款 Paying the Bill with Voucher

Cashier: Good evening, sir. May I help you?

收銀員：晚上好，先生。需要幫忙嗎？

Guest: Yes, I'd like to settle my bill, please. How much is it?

客人：是的，我要買單。一共多少錢？

III. 堂吃酒樓用語 Dine-in Restaurants Expressions

Cashier: Just a moment, please. I'll calculate that for you. Well, your bill comes to $144. 收銀員：請稍候。我替您算一算。嗯，一共是144元。

Guest: Are you sure? It shouldn't be $120?
客人：你確定嗎？不是應該120元嗎？

Cashier: I'm afraid there is a 10% tax and a 10% service charge.
收銀員：恐怕還得加上10%的稅和10%的服務費。

Guest: Well, I see. Can I use this voucher here, please?
客人：哦，我明白了。我可以用這張餐券付款嗎？

Cashier: Sure, sir. Could you sign the voucher here, please?
收銀員：當然可以，先生。請在餐券上簽名。

Guest: Why do I have to sign?　　客人：爲什麼要簽名？

Cashier: I'm afraid the travel agent requires your signature.
收銀員：恐怕旅行社要求有您的簽名。

Guest: I see. Here you are.　　客人：我明白了。給你。

Cashier: Thank you, sir. Please come again.
收銀員：謝謝，先生。請再次光臨。

結賬出錯 Mistakes on the Bills

Cashier: May I help you, sir?　　收銀員：有什麼事嗎，先生？

Guest: Yes, I am afraid you've overcharged me.
客人：是的，恐怕你多算了我的費用。

Cashier: I'm very sorry, sir. May I see your bill, please?
收銀員：對不起，先生。請給我看看您的賬單好嗎？

Guest: Here you are.　　客人：給你賬單。

Cashier: How much change did I give you, sir?
收銀員：我找了多少錢給您，先生？

Guest: You gave me $26 instead of $36.

客人：你找了我26塊而不是36塊。

Cashier: I'm very sorry for the mistake. Here is the right change.

收銀員：很抱歉我弄錯了。這是正確的找零。

Guest: Thank you.

客人：非常感謝。

Cashier: Thanks a lot, sir. Have a nice evening.

收銀員：非常感謝，先生。祝您有個快樂的夜晚。

IV. 自助餐用語
Expressions for Buffet

- ✅ 常用句型 Common Expressions/Sentences
- ✅ 會話關鍵句子 Key Expressions for Serving Guests
- ✅ 埋單結帳常用句子 Key Expressionss While Paying the Bills

IV. 自助餐用語
Expressions for Buffet

常用句型 Common Expressions/Sentences

Enjoy your food and please come back for more food.
請享用你的菜和回來取更多的食物。

Feel free to help yourself. 隨便享用。

Help yourself at the food bar please. 請自己在食物吧取食，

Please use clean plates each time when retuning to the food bar.
每次到食物臺取菜時，請用幹净的碟子。

Please use clean plates each time when retuning to the salad bar. 每次到沙拉吧取菜時，請用幹净的碟子。

The more you have, the happier we are. 你們吃得越多，我們越開心。

There are almost 100 items (dishes) to choose from every day at our restaurant. 我們餐館每天供應接近100種菜式選擇。

We have many kinds of food to choose from. 我們有很多種食物可供選擇。

Why don't you have more? You are paying the same price anyway.
你爲什麼不多吃一點？反正都是同一價錢。

Would you prefer the buffet or the regular order?
你選擇自助餐還是按菜譜點菜呢？

All you can eat for just $8.99. 祇要付$8.99你就可以盡情地享受。

This price includes soda & ice Cream. 這個價格包括汽水和冰淇淋。

Children under age 8 are only half price. 八歲之下的小孩祇要半價。

Every item for lunch is $3.25 per lb, dinner is $4.25 per lb.
午餐的每一種菜是 $3.295一磅，晚餐是 $4.25一磅。

105

IV. 自助餐用語 Expressions for Buffet

I'm afraid you must pay in advance. 我恐怕你要先付錢。

The dinner buffet is $16.95, plus tax; soft drink is included.
自助晚餐是$16.95加稅，飲料包括在內。

There is no extra charge for the refill of drink. 添汽水是免費的。

We charge extra $1.50 for the drink. 我們要另收$1.50汽水錢。

We offer two sizes of soda, small and large, what size would you prefer, sir?
我們提供小與大兩種汽水，先生，你要哪種呢？

You just need to pay $6.99 for the lunch buffet and eat as much as you can.
您祇需要付$6.99就可以盡情享用我們的自助午餐。

Can I fix you another drink? 你還要一些飲料（尤指酒）嗎？

Can I refill the tea for you? 我可以為你添茶嗎？

Do you need a refill for your soda? 你要添點汽水嗎？

Would you like a new plate for your meal? 您想換一個新盤子用餐嗎？

All food at our buffet is sold by the pound.
我們的自助餐食物都按磅出售。

All the dishes we serve are without M.S.G. 我們的菜都沒有用味精。

Any four items with white rice and one soup is for $4.50 0nly.
任選四菜一湯加白飯，祇要$4.50。

Catering available, ask us to cater your next affair.
承辦酒席服務，讓我們為你承辦下一個宴會。

Corporate charge accounts are welcome. 歡迎使用公司團體購。

For faster service, please place your order in advance.
為了更快捷的服務，請預先下單。

Minimum of 50% deposit is required for all party orders.
所有的派對訂單至少需要交50%的定金。

One day advance ordering for parties gets 10% off.

提前一天預定派對可得10%的優惠。

Order $100 or more, get 10% off (For pick up only).

訂購$100或更多的菜可得10%優惠（祇限于自己來拿）。

Please pay first before starting your buffet. 請先付錢再享用自助餐。

Prices and menu are subject to change without prior notice.

價格與菜式可能會改變，不另通知。

Take out is available from the buffet, price by the pound.

自助餐提供外賣，按磅計算。

Tea and coffee are all included in the price. 茶與咖啡已經包括在價格裏。

The Buffet includes a salad bar. 自助餐包括一個沙拉臺。

The Price does not include the sales tax. 價格没有包括銷售稅。

The price doesn't include any soda. 價錢不包括任何汽水。

The price for the buffet includes soda and ice cream.

自助餐的價錢包括汽水和冰淇淋。

We cater to any party including but not limit to Birthday and Wedding.

我們承辦包括生日，婚禮等任何派對酒席。

We have take out order menu on the counter. 在櫃臺上我們有外賣菜單。

We offer party rooms with karaoke. 我們提供帶有卡拉OK的貴賓房。

You can choose what you want yourself from the food bar and we will weigh it for you. 你可以在食物臺那邊選擇你所要的，然后我們稱重及算錢。

You can get what you like from the tray over here by using the take out box.

您可以用外賣盒子在食物盤那邊選擇你所喜歡的食物。

You can order from our regular menu if you do not want to be charged by pound. 如果您不需要按磅定外賣，可以從菜單上點菜。

IV. 自助餐用語 Expressions for Buffet

You can order takeout from the buffet by the pound.
你可以按磅購買自助餐的食物作外賣。

You can pay at your table or the counter after your meal.
用餐后,你可以在座位或櫃臺上付錢。

會話關鍵句子 Key Expressions for Serving Guests

A table for eight is not available, can I put two tables together for you?
我們沒有八個位的桌子,我可把兩張桌子拼起來給你嗎?

Are you still serving the lunch buffet? 還提供自助午餐嗎?

Children 2 years old or under are $3.00. 兩歲或兩歲以下的兒童$3.00。

Children between 3 and 5 are $3.50. 三歲到五歲之間的兒童$3.50。

Children between 6 and 12 are half price.
六歲到十二歲之間的兒童為成人的半價。

Dinner buffet has more food than the lunch buffet and usually we serve lobster and other sea foods. 自助晚餐的食物比午餐多,而且常在晚餐都提供龍蝦以及其他海鮮。

Do you want the buffet or to order from our regular menu?
你要自助餐還是按菜單點菜呢?

Do you like that table which is close the food bar?
你喜歡靠近食物臺的那張桌子嗎?

Do you prefer Smoking or non-smoking area? 抽烟區還是不抽烟區?

Do you smoke? 您抽烟嗎?

Do you want to take a look at the food on the bar first?
你要先看看臺上的食物嗎?

Four adults and two kids, right? 四個成人兩個兒童,對嗎?

How many of you, sir? 先生,你們共有幾位?

How old is she? 她多少歲了？

I'm afraid it's too late for dinner buffet now. Would you like to order something from our regular menu? We can give you a 15% off in this case. 我恐怕自助晚餐的時間已經太遲了，你要不要在一般的菜單中點一些菜？我們可以給你15%的優惠。

I'm afraid this food is cold; I think the fresh food will be here soon. 恐怕這些食物已經冷了，我想新的菜馬上就來了。

I'm sorry, the smoking section is full. Do you want to wait for a table? Or sit in the non-smoking section?
對不起，吸煙區已經滿了，你要等座位還是要禁煙區？

Is the lunch buffet still being served? 還提供自助午餐嗎？

Is the price different for adults and kids? 成人與兒童的價格不同嗎？

Our buffet will close in 30 minutes. If you want anything more, please get it as soon as possible. 對不起，還有30分鐘自助餐就收餐了。如果您還需要點什麼，請早點取用。

She is about 4 years old? 她差不多4歲了？

The bread is home-made. 面包是自制的。

The buffet is not ready yet, can you wait for a couple of minutes？
自助餐還沒有好，你可以等幾分鐘嗎？

The dinner buffet is over, we're going to clean the trays now, and the food is cold. However, you can take a look at the food bar first, and tell me what you want. We can prepare it for you and send the food to your table.
自助晚餐已經停止了，菜也冷了。我們將準備清洗食物盤但是你可以先到食物臺中看看再告訴我你所要的，然后我們單獨為你做及送到你的桌上。

The dressings are all over the table. 桌子上到處都是調味醬。

IV. 自助餐用語 Expressions for Buffet

The lunch buffet has changed to the dinner buffet already.
自助午餐已經改為自助晚餐了。

The non-smoking area is full now, would you mind sitting in the smoking area for a few minutes first until the non-smoking become available？禁煙區已經滿了，你介意先坐在吸煙區一會兒，然后再轉到禁烟區嗎？

The trash can is over there. 垃圾桶在那邊。

We have 3 prices for children during lunch buffet.
我們提供的兒童自助午餐有三種價格。

We have a vegetable and fruit salad bar over there.
在那邊，我們有蔬菜色拉和水果色拉吧。

We need more chicken wings on the buffet. 自助餐需要再添些鷄翅。

We serve the buffet at lunch time only. 我們祇在午餐時間提供自助餐。

We're out of pasta. 我們的意大利面沒有了。

We're closed at 10:00 PM, but last serving for buffet is 9:30PM.
我們是10點關門，但是提供自助晚餐的最后時間是 9:30PM。

What's the difference between lunch buffet and dinner buffet?
自助午餐與自助晚餐有什麼不同？

You just leave it on the table; we'll take care of that.
你祇要把它留在桌上，我們會清理的。

情景對話 Situatianal Dialogues

情景對話 I Dialogue I

W=Waiter 服務生 C=Customer 顧客

W: Welcome to Buffet City. How can I help you?
服務生：歡迎來到自助城。我能幫您做什麼呢？

C: I'd like to know what your buffet is like.

顧客：我想知道您們的自助餐是什麼樣的。

W: It's got an extensive salad bar.

服務生：我們有一個品種豐富的沙拉臺。

C: Do you have hot and cold salads? 顧客：你們有熱沙拉和冷沙拉嗎？

W: Yes, and we have a wide variety of salad dressings to choose from.

服務生：有，還有許多沙拉醬可以選擇。

C: Do you have any soup? 顧客：您們有湯嗎？

W: Yes, we have three different kinds of soup today.

服務生：有，今天我們有三種湯。

C: What kind of soup do you have? 顧客：都是什麼湯？

W: Today, we have creamy tomato, spicy bean and onion soup.

服務生：今天我們有奶油西紅柿湯，辣豆湯和洋蔥湯。

C: What kind of main meals do you have on your buffet?

顧客：自助餐的主食都有什麼？

W: We have Steak, Lobster, Sushi, Pizza and Pasta.

服務生：我們有披薩，意大利面和滷汁面條。

C: How about sides? 顧客：配菜呢？

W: We have French fries, cheese bread and chicken wings.

服務生：我們有炸薯條，奶酪面包和鷄翅。

C: That sounds goods. We'll take two.

顧客：聽起來不錯，我們兩位在這兒吃了。

情景對話 II Dialogue II

W=Waiter 服務生 C=Customer 顧客

W: How is everything here? 服務生：這的菜怎麼樣？

C: Great. We're really enjoying the buffet.

顧客：非常好。我們真的很喜歡這裏的自助餐。

IV. 自助餐用語 Expressions for Buffet

W: Are you finished with these plates? 服務生：這些盤子用完了嗎？

C: Yes, except for this one. I'm still working on it. 顧客：是的，除了這個盤子其它的都用完了。這個盤子的，我還在吃。

W: Would you mind if I took the rest of these plates away?
服務生：您介意我把其他盤子撤走嗎？

W: Not at all. 服務生：不介意。

C: Would you like me to bring you new ones for your next trip to the buffet?
顧客：你希望我給您再拿幾個新盤子嗎？以便下次去取食物。

C: Yes, please. That would be great.
顧客：好的。那太好了。

W: Can I get you anything else right now?
服務生：您現在還要其他什麼嗎？

C: Actually, the last time we went up, we noticed that the French fries were running low.
顧客：嗯，上次我們去取食物的時候，看到炸薯條快沒了。

W: Thanks for letting me know. I'll go and get some more. I can bring you a few slices for you if you prefer.
服務生：謝謝您告訴我，我去再加一些。如果您願意的話我給您拿幾片過來放在桌上。

C: That won't be necessary. Thanks though.
顧客：不用了，非常感謝。

埋單結帳常用句子 Key Expressions While Paying the Bills

Waiter, check please. 服務生，請給帳單。

You may pay at the table. 你可以就在桌面上付錢。

Whose check shall I put for the soda? 要我把汽水記在誰的賬單上？

You can pay to the cashier at the counter as you go out.

出去時，可以在櫃臺收銀員那裏付錢。

Would you like a breakdown of the bill? 您的賬面要細分嗎？

Sorry, we don't accept credit card or check.

對不起，我們不收信用卡和支票。

I'm sorry, I forgot to charge you for the soda．

對不起，我忘記算你可樂的錢。

The price of our buffet is $22.00 for one person, with a 15% service charge. We'll give a 50% discount for children under 4 feet. 我們自助餐的收費是每位22美元，另外再加10%的服務費。4尺以下的兒童按50%收費。

Only coffee and tea are included in buffet. If you want something else to drink, you will need to pay for it.

自助餐祇包茶和咖啡，其他飲品需要另外收費。

I'm sorry. Cappuccino is not included in buffet. Do you mind paying extra?

對不起，卡布奇諾不包括在自助餐裏，您介不介意另外付費呢？

I'm afraid there are a 15% service charge and 8.75% sale tax. 恐怕還得加上15%服務費和8.75%銷售稅。

Your bill includes a 10% service charge and a 8% sale tax. 您的賬單包括10%的服務費和8%的銷售稅。

V. 酒吧服務
Bar Service

- ✅ 酒吧服務要點 Bar Service Key Points
- ✅ 常用句型表達 Useful Expressions
- ✅ 情景對話 Situational Dialogues

一、酒吧服務要點 Bar Service Key Points

1. 所有飲料應用右手從客人的右側服務（在不打擾客人和保證安全的情況下）。爲了避免發生意外，當服務員拿着飲料在客人身後時，應提醒客人。"Excuse me, sir/madam."（對不起，先生/女士。）

2. 在不打擾客人的情況下，呈送和添加飲料時要報名稱。"Here is your Bloody Mary, sir/madam." (您的雪瑪莉，先生/女士。)當知道客人姓名時，就要稱呼他的名字。

3. 在拿走空杯之前一定要問客人是否需要另一杯飲料。"Would you like another one?"(您需要再來一杯嗎?)

4. 客人之間講話時不要側身細聽，也不要插話。不可催促客人飲酒，也不可因 客人飲得過多、或太少、或時間太長而流露出不耐煩的情緒。

5. 熱情接待所有客人，不厚此薄彼。客人喝醉了也不能有輕慢的態度。酒醉的 客人離桌，應暫留其物品原樣，以備核查。

二、常用句型表達 Useful Expressions

A night-cap before retiring, sir? 先生，臨睡前喝一杯怎麼樣？

Could you give me the soft drink list, I don't drink at all. 能把飲料單給我看看嗎？我不喝酒。

Do you accept this credit card? 你們接受這張信用卡嗎？

Excuse me, sir. There is alcohol in the special drink. Maybe not fit for the kids. 先生，這些特飲是含酒精的，或許對小孩不太合適。

Frankly speaking, I don't like this wine. 老實說，我不喜歡這種酒。

Has this wine really been preserved for years?
這種酒真的是陳年葡萄酒嗎？

Have a nice trip home. 歸途愉快。

V. 酒吧服務 Bar Service

The base of Old Fashioned cocktail is whiskey.

古典雞尾酒的基酒是威士忌。

Here is the drink list, sir. Please take your time.

先生，這是酒單，請慢慢看。

How about another half, sir?

再來一杯怎樣？

How about Apple Martini, if you don't like this drink?

如果您不喜歡這個，試試蘋果馬爹利怎麼樣？

How about one for the road? 臨走前再喝一杯，好嗎？

How much do all these come to? 這些共計多少錢？

I have another waiting on ice for you.

我還爲您準備了另外一杯呢

I'm afraid not. 我想恐怕不行。

I want to look through the wine list first. 我想先看看酒水單。

I'd like to try something typically American Wine.

我想試試地道的美國紅酒。

I'm afraid it is not possible. 這恐怕不行。

I'm really sorry. I'd like to oblige, but you see my difficulty.

非常抱歉。我很願意幫忙，但是希望您能夠體諒我。

Only half a glass will be fine I'm not really a drinker.

一半就可以了，我不是很會喝酒。

Our drinks are half price from 5 p.m. to 8 p.m., would you like one more?

下午5點至8點，我們的飲料半價出售，請問您要再來一杯嗎？

Our licensing laws are quite strict. Nobody under 18 years of age is allowed in a bar.

我們的牌照條例非常嚴格，任何18歲以下的孩子都不能進入酒吧。

Please say "when", sir. 先生,請您告訴我什麼時候停。

Please give me a receipt. 請給我一張發票。

Please give me another drink. 請給我另一份飲料。

Please wait a moment. 請稍等一下。

Regretfully not. 很抱歉,不行。

Sorry, sir. Any drink served cannot be changed or returned, unless there is a mistake. 對不起,先生,除非出現錯誤,否則任何售出的酒水都不能退換。

Straight up, sir? 要純的嗎,先生?

Thank you for your coming, good-bye. 謝謝您的光臨,再見。

The same again, sir? 先生,同樣的再來一杯怎樣?

The bar is full now. Do you care to wait for about 20 minutes?

酒吧現在客滿,請稍等約20分鐘好嗎?

The children are too young to drink wine. 孩子太小還不能喝酒。

There is a show in our lobby bar. Would you like to see it?

大堂酒吧裏有表演,您願意去看嗎?

We don't like soda. What kind of juice do you have?

我們不喜歡蘇打水(汽水)。有什麼果汁嗎?

We have some soft drinks for the ladies. 請給女士們一些飲料吧。

We have a bottle of wine that has been preserved for twenty years.

我們有一瓶保存了20年的葡萄酒。

We serve many kinds of drinks. Please help yourself.

我們供應很多種飲料,請自便。

Welcome to our bar. 歡迎光臨我們的酒吧。

We're about finish. No more wine for us.

我們已經差不多了,不要再加酒了。

V. 酒吧服務 Bar Service

What can I offer you, ladies and gentlemen?
先生們、女士們，請問需要些什麼？

What is your pleasure, sir? 您喜歡什麼，先生？

What would you like to drink? The same as usual, Mr. Smith?
您要喝點什麼，史密斯先生？照往常的嗎？

With or without ice, sir? 加冰嗎，先生？

Would you bring me one orange juice and one soda for her?
請給我拿一杯橙汁和給她拿一杯蘇打水。

Would you like to try another kind of our new style? It is very popular after launched. 您是否試試我們的新推介？它推出以後一直很受歡迎。

Would you like to try our house wine? 您試試我們的店酒如何？

Would you care for a glass of sherry with your Chicken Fingers?
在吃雞爪的時候是否要一杯雪利酒？

Would you like me to call a taxi for you? 要我為您叫出租車嗎？

Would you like to have cocktail or whisky on the rocks?
您要雞尾酒還是要威士忌加冰？

Would you mind if I smoke? 你不介意我抽支烟吧？

You see I'm doing my duty. 您知道，我祇是在履行職責。

You tried our house wine last time. How about this time? We have something new. 上回您已經試過我們的店酒了，這回您想要什麼？我們有一些新的酒。

情景對話 Situational Dialogues

招呼客人 Serving Guests

B=Barman / Bartender 酒吧服務員　G1=Guest 1 顧客1　G2=Guest 2 顧客2

B: Good evening, sir. What can I do for you?

B: 晚上好！請問有什麼可以爲您效勞？

G1: I'd like a drink.　　　　　G1: 我要喝勁大點的酒。

G2: Me too. Give me a double whisky and soda.

G2: 我也是。 我要雙份威士忌加蘇打水。

B: We serve brandy, whisky, vodka and so on. What would you like? (To guest 2) How would you like the whisky, straight or on the rocks?

B: 我們有白蘭地、威士忌、伏特加等，您要哪一種？（轉向另外一個客人）您要哪一種，加冰還是不加冰？

G1: Without ice. Ice will spoil the taste.

G1: 不加冰。加冰就把味道破壞了。

B: Straight away, sir.　B: 馬上就好。

G2: I'm suffering from a cold.　G2: 我正患感冒。

B: Then I recommend the vodka swizzle. It is made from several liquors and mixed into vermouth. B: 那我推薦您喝伏特加鷄尾酒。它由幾種烈酒配制而成，最後加入苦艾酒。

G2: That sounds wonderful. G2: 那聽起來不錯。

G1&G2: We must be off now. G1&G2: 我們得走了。

B: How about one for the road? B: 喝一杯再走吧。

G1&G2: Why not? The same again, please.

G1&G2: 好呀！同樣的再來一杯吧。

對客人說 "不" Say "No" to Guests

B=Barman 酒吧服務員　　G=Guest 顧客

B: Good evening! Welcome to the One Way Bar.

B: 晚上好！歡迎光臨單行道酒吧。

G: Can our two children come in to listen to some music for a moment?

119

V. 酒吧服務　Bar Service

G: 我能把我的兩個孩子帶進來聽聽音樂嗎？

B: How old are they, sir?

B: 他們多大了，先生？

G: John is ten and May is six.

G: 約翰10歲，梅6歲。

B: I'm afraid not sir. Our licensing laws are quite strict. Nobody under 18 years of age is allowed in a bar.

B: 我想恐怕不行。我們的牌照條例非常嚴格，任何18歲以下的孩子都不能進入酒吧。

G: I know, but we thought since they're on holiday, it won't be any harm. And I won't order them anything strong. Maybe they will just dance a bit. It's our last night in Florida.

G: 我知道，但是我想他們正在度假，不會有什麼害處，而且我也不會給他們點任何烈性飲料的。他們可能祇是會跳跳舞。這是我們在佛羅裏達的最後一個晚上。

B: I'm really sorry. I'd like to oblige but you see my difficulty. Now how about a drink in the lounge outside? You can see the band and listen to the music as well.

B: 非常抱歉。我很願意幫忙，但是希望您能夠體諒我。請兩個小朋友在外面的休息室喝飲料怎麼樣？在那兒也可以看到樂隊表演和聽到音樂的。

G: Well, you're only doing your duty.

G: 好吧。你也是在盡自己的責任。

VI. 宴會
Banquet

- ✅ 宴會預訂 Banquet Reservations
- ✅ 爲公司宴會做準備 Preparing a Company Banquet
- ✅ 準備婚宴 Preparing a Wedding Banquet
- ✅ 準備生日宴會 Preparing a Birthday Banquet

VI. 宴會 Banquet

1. 宴會預訂 Banquet Reservations

常用句子表達 Useful Expressions

招呼客人 Serving Guests

A deposit of $200 is required to secure your booking. 爲確保您的預訂，請付押金$200塊。

Could you tell me the minimum charge for a 200-person dinner? 您能否告訴我200人宴會的最低收費是多少？

"Cash on delivery" means the guests pay the drinks themselves. In short we call it "C.O.D." 由來客自付飲料費用"需要客人自己支付所需的酒水費用，簡稱"C.O.D."。

"Open bar on fixed price" means the guests can drink freely during the fixed hour within the fixed price.
"在預先定時定價範圍內客人自由享用"是指客人在預定的時間及預訂的價錢範圍內可以自由享受各種酒水。

Excuse me, sir/madam. Can I change a new plate for you? 先生/夫人，請讓我爲您換一個新的碟子好嗎？

Excuse me. Can I have another bowl of soup?
服務員，可以再給我一碗湯嗎？

How do you charge for the drinks? 您們的酒水是如何收費的？

How many tables shall we arrange? 請問我們應該安排多少張臺呢？

How much would you like to spend for each table?
請問每張臺的費用標準是多少？

How would you like us to arrange the tables? 您喜歡我們怎樣擺桌子呢？

I'd like to give my friend a proper farewell. What would you recommend?
我想爲我的朋友安排一個告別宴會，請問有什麼推薦？

Is everything satisfactory? 請問您對我們餐廳還滿意嗎？

It's quite common for the organizer to pay for all the drinks for his guests, with no limit. This is called "on consumption to master account". 通常組織者會無限制地支付來賓得所有酒水費用。這稱爲"客人隨意消費計入總賬，由主人包付"。

Please feel free to contact us if you have any questions with the payment arrangements. 如果您對結算方式有什麼疑問，歡迎隨時與我們聯系。

Please have a drink in the lounge. The banquet will begin in 20 minutes. 請在休息室喝杯飲料。宴會20分鐘後就開始。

Please separate this fish for us. 請幫我們分一下這條魚。

The minimum charge for a 200-person dinner is $6,000, excluding drinks. 200人的宴會最低收費是$6,000，不包括酒水。

The soup is ready, please enjoy it. 湯已經準備好了，請慢用！

We are very satisfied with your preparations. Thank you. 我們對您們的準備工作非常滿意。謝謝。

We can arrange all kinds of banquets for you. 我們可以爲您提供各種宴會服務。

We need some slap-up food and beverage for the banquet. What can you offer? 這次宴會我們想要一些高檔的飯菜，您們可以提供什麼呀？

We'd like to have the banquet hail decorated. It would be better if a Christmas tree stands in the middle with some colorful streamers. 我們想把宴會廳裝飾一番。如果能在大廳中央放一顆帶有彩色垂帶的聖誕樹就更好了。

Welcome to ABC Restaurant. Are you here for the Farewell Banquet? 歡迎光臨ABC餐廳。請問您是參加退休宴會的嘉賓嗎？

We'll get everything ready in advance. 我們會準備好一切。

VI. 宴會 Banquet

What drinks would you like? 請問您想要什麼的酒水呢?

What kinds of fruit / dessert would you like? 您想要些什麼水果/甜品呢?

What size of party are you going to order and how many people will attend the birthday party in our restaurant? 您想在我們餐廳辦一個多大規模的生日會呢，大概會有多少人參加?

What will you prepare for our banquet?
你們會為我們的宴會準備些什麼呀?

Would you like us to serve the food now? 請問現在可以開始上菜嗎?

You may serve the dessert now. Remember to put the birthday cake before the girl in red. 您可以開始上甜點了。 請留意把生日蛋糕擺在那個穿紅衣服的女孩面前。

宴會預訂對話 Banquet Reservation Dialogue

R = Reservation Clerk 宴會預訂員　　G=Guest 顧客

G: Hello, is this the Hudson River Village Restaurant?
G: 您好，請問這是哈德森村莊嗎?

R: Speaking. May I help you?　R：是的，需要效勞嗎?

G: Yes. This is Jackson White from the ABC Accounting Firm. We'd like to have a farewell party banquet in your restaurant. Can you arrange it for us?
G: 您好！我是ABC會計師樓的杰克森，懷特。我們想在貴酒樓舉行一個告別宴會，您們能夠為我們安排一下嗎?

R: Certainly, Mr. White. When would you like your banquet?
R: 當然可以。請問宴會什麼時候舉行?

G: At 7:00 P.M. tomorrow.　G: 明天晚上7點鐘。

R: How many people will there be in your party?　R: 請問一共有多少人?

G: There will be 50 altogether. G: 總共50人。

R: Then I will arrange five tables for you. Could I recommend the Hudson View - the newly decorated hall? It's well equipped and spacious. I'm sure it's suitable for a company banquet and you will like it.
R: 那我就幫您安排5張桌子吧。在新裝修的哈德森河景廳怎麼樣？那設備齊全，而且很寬敞。我覺得很適合開公司宴會，相信您會喜歡。

G: That sounds great! We'll take it!
G: 聽起來不錯。我們就訂這一間了。

R: Then how much would you like to spend for each table?
R: 請問每周臺的費用標準定在多少？

G: About $800 dollars and make the dishes typically Chinese. Besides, this banquet is given in honor of Mr. Morse, who used to be our marketing manager, and now will be the executive manager in another district. I think we need to prepare something special for him.
G: 每臺$800，要正宗的中國菜。另外，這個宴會是爲莫爾斯先生送行的，他曾經是我們的市場部經理，現在要高就另一地區的總經理了。我看得爲他準備些特別的東西。

R: Certainly. How about "Good Fortune Roasted Whole Baby Pig"? It's a baby pig roasted with our House Sauce. R: 好的。來一條幸運烤整乳猪怎麼樣？ 那是本地秘制醬料的紅燒乳猪。

G: Great! It will be perfect for our farewell banquet.
G: 好主意！ 這道菜非常適合我們這個告別晚宴。

R: That's fine. How about drinks?
R: 好的，需要什麼酒水嗎？

G: Please prepare some Dry Wine, Budweiser Beer and Champagne.
G: 請準備一些幹白葡萄酒，百威啤酒和香檳。

VI. 宴會 Banquet

R: All right. What kind of fruit would you like?

R: 好的,需要些什麼水果?

G: Please prepare some watermelon, apples, oranges, pineapples and grapes.

G: 請準備一些西瓜,蘋果,橙子,菠蘿和葡萄。

R: OK. So let me repeat what you've ordered: a farewell banquet in Hudson River View Hall at 7:00 P.M. tomorrow; fives tables for 50 people, each table about $800; drinks and fruit; a special dish of "Good Fortune Roasted Whole Baby Pig" for each table. Is that correct, Mr. White?

R: 好的。讓我為您復述一次您點的單:告別晚會明天晚上7點在哈德森河景廳舉行;5圍臺50個人;每臺按約$800的標準;需要水果和酒水;每臺有一道特別菜肴:"幸運烤整乳豬"。對嗎,懷特先生?

G: Yes. That's right.

G: 是的。沒錯。

R: Thank you, Mr. White. We'll get everything ready before the banquet. I hope you'll enjoy it.   R: 謝謝您,懷特先生。我們一定會在宴會前準備好一切,希望您們喜歡。

G: Thank you very much. Good-bye!   G: 非常感謝!再見。

2. 為公司宴會做準備 Preparing a Company Banquet

常用句子表達 Useful Expressions

How many guests are you planning for? 您預計有多少客人?

How many tables would you like? 您想要多少桌?

Are you planning on having any entertainment? 您打算安排娛樂表演嗎?

Do you need a host? 您需要主持人嗎?

Do you need any microphones? 您需要麥克風嗎?

Would you like some music? 您想來點音樂嗎?

Would you like a karaoke system set up for the banquet?

您需要給宴會準備一個卡拉OK系統嗎？

What is your standard banquet menu? 您的標準的宴會菜單是什麼？

We recommend about 15 dishes for each table. 我們推薦每桌15道菜。

Would you like Chinese wine or Western wine?

您喜歡中國酒還是西方的葡萄酒？

What date are you looking at for the banquet? 您考慮幾號安排宴會？

What time do you want to start the banquet? 您想要宴會什麼時間開始？

情景對話 1 Situational Dialogue 1

M=Manager 經理　C=Customer 顧客

Manager: How can I help you? 經理：我能為您做什麼呢？

Customer: I'd like to organize a company banquet.

顧客：我想安排公司的宴會。

M: What date are you looking at? M: 您考慮在哪一天？

C: The 20th of December. C: 12月20號。

M: What time did you want to start? M: 想幾點開始？

C: 6:00 p.m. C: 晚上6點。

M: How many guests are you planning for? M: 您預計有多少客人？

C: There will be about 100 guests. C: 大約一百人吧。

M: So, how about ten tables? M: 那10桌怎麼樣？

C: That would be fine. C: 不錯。

M: Have you thought about having any entertainment?

M: 考慮安排娛樂表演嗎？

C: Does your restaurant provide any? C: 你們餐廳能提供嗎？

M: We have singers and dancers who often perform at banquets.

M: 我們有歌手和舞蹈演員，他們常常在宴會上表演。

VI. 宴會 Banquet

C: Would it be possible to see a sample performance before we book them?

C: 在預定之前是否能看一場示範表演呢?

M: Certainly. We have a sample performance on our website that you can view. M: 當然可以。在我們的網站上您可以瀏覽示範表演。

C: Great. C: 太好了。

情景對話 2 Dialogue 2

M=Manager 經理　C=Customer 顧客

Manager: Have you put some more thought into the banquet menu?

經理：您對宴會菜單還有更多的想法嗎？

Customer: Yes, I have. 顧客：是的。

M: Let's talk about it. M: 首先我們談談飲料吧。　C: OK.　C: 好。

M: Do you want t to have Chinese wine or Western wine?

M: 你們想喝中國酒還是西方的葡萄酒？

C: Chinese wine. C: 中國酒。

M: What other beverage would you like? M: 別的飲料還想要點什麼？

C: Beer, juice, and Sprite. C: 啤酒、果汁和雪碧。

M: How about tea? M: 茶呢？

C: Green tea and eight treasure tea, please. C: 來綠茶和八寶茶。

M: OK, now the food. Would you like Menu A, B, or C?

M: 好的，現在說說菜，您想用A套餐，B套餐還是C套。

C: Menu A. C: A套餐。

M: That's a great choice. Do you have any changes that you'd like to make to that menu? M: 選得好。您想對這個套餐做些調整嗎？

C: Actually, would it possible to substitute sweet and sour fish for the steamed sea bass? C: 實際上，您能把糖醋魚換成清蒸鱸魚嗎？

M: That's not a problem. M: 沒問題。

3. 準備婚宴 Preparing a Wedding Banquet

常用句子表達 Useful Expressions

Do you hold wedding banquets? 您舉辦婚宴嗎?

I'd like to hold a wedding banquet for my son. 我想爲兒子舉辦婚宴。

If the bride and groom have decided on a song for their first dance, let us know ahead of time.
如果新郎、新娘決定了第一支舞的舞曲，請提前告訴我們。

If you would like to bring additional decorations, we can hang them up for you. 如果你願意帶額外的裝飾，我們可以給你們挂上。

The MC will announce the couple and introduce the relatives.
司儀會宣布新人到場，并介紹親戚。

The rooms come with basic wedding decorations.
房間配有基本的結婚裝飾。

We can also provide an MC for the event.
我們也可以爲這次活動提供司儀。

We can offer champagne for the toasts. 我們能提供香檳敬酒。

We can organize a band, a DJ and background music. 我們可以安排一支樂隊，一個音樂節目主持人和背景音樂。

We can provide a wedding cake and wedding sweets.
我們能够提供結婚蛋糕和喜糖。

We can provide you with a wedding photographer.
我們可以提供婚禮攝像師。

Would you like to have some entertainment? 您喜歡有娛樂表演嗎?

Would you like us to announce the couple?
您願意由我們來宣布新人到場嗎?

VI. 宴會 Banquet

情景對話 1 Situational Dialogue 1

R=Receptionist 招待員 C=Customer 顧客

R: Paradise Hotel and Restaurant, this is Jenny speaking. How may I help you?

招待員：天堂酒店，我是珍妮，我能爲您做點什麼？

C: I'd like to organize a wedding banquet for my son. Do you offer wedding banquet services?

顧客：我想爲我的兒子安排婚宴。您們能提供婚宴服務嗎？

R: We certainly do. What date would you like?

招待員：當然能。你想哪一天辦？

C: The 21st of April. 顧客：4月21日。

R: That's fine. We have a few rooms still available.

招待員：行。我們還有幾個場地可用。

C: That's great. I know it's a busy time for wedding banquets.

顧客：太好了，我知道現在是婚宴的忙季。

R: How many guests will you have? 招待員：您會有多少客人？

C: Approximately 300 guests. 顧客：接近三百人吧。

R: We can offer you the Oak Room then, which is a mid-sized holds up to 400 guests.

招待員：我們到時可爲您提供橡木廳，中等大小，能容納400人。

C: OK. 顧客：好的。

R: Would you like to book an appointment with the manager to discuss the banquet in more detail?

招待員：您想和經理預約個時間再談談細節上的問題嗎？

C: Yes, please.

顧客：是的，請。

情景對話 2 Situational Dialogue 2：

M=Manager 經理 C=Customer 顧客

M: Hi James, how are you? 經理：你好，詹姆斯，最近怎麼樣？

C: Fine, thanks. 顧客：很好，謝謝。

M: So, it looks like you are organizing a wedding banquet for your son. Is that right? 經理：你好像在給兒子安排婚宴，是嗎？

C: Yes. We're very excited about that. 顧客：是的，我們都為此非常興奮。

M: As you should be. Weddings are very special days indeed. Now, let's talk about the entertainment. What did you have in mind?
經理：應該這樣。婚禮確實是個特殊的日子。現在我們談談娛樂表演。你有什麼想法嗎？

C: Well, my son is in a band and would like them to perform. Is that possible? 顧客：嗯，我兒子在樂隊工作，他想讓他們來表演，可以嗎？

M: Of course. As you can see, we have quite a large stage and dance floor here in the Oak Room. Now, how about an MC? Did you have someone in mind for that?
經理：當然，你都看到了，我們的橡木廳有一個很大的舞臺和舞池。現在談談司儀，你想好讓誰當司儀了嗎？

C: If you could provide an MC, that'd be great.
顧客：如果你們要是能提供司儀，那就太好了。

M: We certainly can. What we'll do beforehand is to have the MC meet with your son and future daughter-in-law so that he can learn more about who they are as a couple.
經理：我們當然可以，那我們事先要做的就是讓司儀與你兒子和未來的兒媳談談，以便讓他更了解這對新婚夫婦。

C: That's great. 顧客：好極了。

VI. 宴會 Banquet

4. 準備生日宴會 Preparing a Birthday Banquet

常用句子表達 Useful Expressions

Also, we can provide the birthday girl with a complimentary birthday bag.
同時，我們可以爲過生日的女孩提供一個免費的生日袋。

Are the guests' family, friends or both?
客人都是親戚，朋友還是兩者都有？

Can you provide streamers and balloons?
你能提供橫幅和氣球嗎？

How old is she? 她多大了？

I'd like to hold a birthday banquet for my daughter.
我想爲我女兒舉辦生日宴會。

It's a chocolate birthday cake. 這是巧克力生日蛋糕。

It's her 16th birthday. 這是她16歲生日。

The birthday girl will receive a complimentary bowl of longevity noodles.
過生日的女孩會得到一碗免費的長壽麵。

We can also provide complimentary candles for the birthday cake.
我們還可以贈送生日蠟燭。

We can provide birthday party favors for the guests.
我們可以爲客人們提供生日晚會禮物。

We can provide typical party games if you like.
如果你喜歡，我們可以提供特定的宴會遊戲。

We can set up a table for the gifts.
我們可以支一張桌子放禮物。

Who is the birthday girl? 過生日的女孩是誰？

Would you like some balloons? 您喜歡氣球嗎？

情景對話 1 Situational Dialogue 1

> M=Manager 經理　C=Customer 顧客

M: How can I help you?

經理：我能為您做點什麼？

C: I'd like to hold a birthday banquet for my daughter.

顧客：我想為我女兒舉辦生日宴會。

M: How old is she going to be?　經理：她多大了？

C: It's going to be her sweet 16.

顧客：她就要進入16歲的花季了。

M: That's a very special age, isn't it?

經理：確實是個特別的年紀，不是嗎？

C: Yes, it is.

顧客：是的。

M: When would you like to hold the banquet?

經理：您想什麼時候舉辦生日宴會？

C: Ideally, we'd like to hold it on her birthday, which is May 8th.

顧客：最好能在她的生日那天5月8日。

M: Let me just check and see if that date is available. It looks like we have a banquet that afternoon, but the evening is still available. What time do you want to start the banquet?

經理：我查看一下那天是不是可以，好像那天下午我們有宴會。晚上可以，您想什麼時候開始？

C: How about 7 p.m?

顧客：晚上7點可以嗎？

M: OK. I'll book you in for that date and time for now.

經理：好的，我暫時給您訂在5月8號的晚上7點。

133

VI. 宴會 Banquet

情景對話 2 Situational Dialogue 2

M=Manager 經理 C=Customer 顧客

Customer: I'd like to ask you some questions about the services you provide for birthday banquets.
顧客：我想就生日宴會你們能提供哪些服務提些問題。

Manager: OK. 經理：好的。

C: Do you provide entertainment? 顧客：你們有提供娛樂表演嗎？

M: Yes, we can provide DJs, live bands, and background music. 經理：有的，我們可以提供音樂節目主持人、現場樂隊表演和背景音樂。

C: Do you provide birthday cakes? 顧客：你們有提供生日蛋糕嗎？

M: Yes, we have a fantastic baker on staff that bakes amazing birthday cakes. 經理：有的，我們有一個很棒的面包師，他做的生日蛋糕好得讓人不敢相信。

C: Do you provide birthday candles with the cake?
顧客：你們提供生日蛋糕的蠟燭嗎？

M: We provide complimentary birthday candles with the purchase of a birthday cake.
經理：凡是購買生日蛋糕的，我們都免費提供生日蠟燭。

C: How about birthday decorations? 顧客：裝飾品呢？

M: We have a wide variety of birthday balloons and streamers appropriate for people at any age.
經理：我們有各種生日氣球以及適合各個年齡段的橫幅。

C: OK, I think that's all the questions I have for now. Thanks for your time.
顧客：好的。目前就這麼多問題，占用了你的時間，謝謝。

M: You're welcome. 經理：不客氣。

VII. 日本餐
Japanese Foods

- ✔ 日本料理烹調原則 Cooking Guidelines for Japanese Cuisine
- ✔ 日本料理三大類別 Uniqueness of Japanese Cuisine
- ✔ 日本料理的烹調特色 Types of Japanese Cuisine
- ✔ 日本料理常見的菜單 Common Dishes

- ✔ 醬料 Sauce
- ✔ 沙律 Salad
- ✔ 天婦羅 Tempura
- ✔ 燒烤類 Broiled Dishes
- ✔ 壽司卷 Sushi Roll
- ✔ 飯類 Donburi Rice
- ✔ 其它菜單 Other Dishes

- ✔ 前菜 Appetizer
- ✔ 面類 Noodles
- ✔ 生魚片 Sashimi (Raw Fish)
- ✔ 湯 Soups
- ✔ 菜單講解 Dishes Explanation
- ✔ 常用句子 Useful Sentences
- ✔ 套餐 Set Courses

VII.日本餐　Japanese Foods

日本餐
Japanese Foods

隨着日本經濟的急劇擴張，日本生活方式也逐漸向世界各地擴散。作爲世界美食中的一員，日本料理自然在各國落地生根了。日本菜的口味和飲食方式也開始廣被接受。清淡、不油膩、精致、營養、着重視覺、味覺與器皿之搭配是日本料理的特色。

日本料理烹調原則：

五味	甘	甜	酸	苦	辣
五色	白	黑	黃	紅	綠
五法	生	煮	烤	蒸	炸

日本料理三大類別：

1、本膳料理─傳統正式日本料理

源自室町時代（約十四世紀），是日本理法制度下的產物。現在正式的「本膳料理」已不多見，大約祇出現在少數的正式場合，如婚喪喜慶、成年儀式及祭典宴會上，菜色由五菜二湯到七菜三湯不等。

2、懷石料理－－高級料理

[懷石]的由來是禮師們在進行修行與斷食中，強忍饑餓，而懷抱溫熱的石頭取暖得名。懷石料理原本是搭配茶道，將茶的美味發揮出來的料理，現今已儼然成爲高級料理的代名詞。

3、會席料理－－宴會料理

會席料理不像本膳及懷石料理那麼嚴謹，吃法較自由，除注重美味以外，以較輕鬆的方式享用宴會料理。

日本料理的烹調特色：

　　日本料理烹調的特色着重自然的原味， [原味]是日本料理首要的精神。其烹調方式，十分細膩精致，從數小時慢火熬制的高湯、調味與烹調手法，均以保留食物的原味為前提。

日本料理的美味秘訣，基本上是以糖、醋、味精、醬油、柴魚、昆布等為主要的調味料，除了品嘗香味以外，味覺，觸覺、視覺、嗅覺等亦不容忽視。

日本料理常見的菜單類別大概可以分為下列五種：

（一）生魚片：

　　即是[刺身]，有人直接音譯為「沙西米」。刺身是將新鮮的魚或是貝肉，依照適當的刀法切成，享用時佐以醬油與山葵泥(Wasabi)調和之沾醬的一種生食料理。

　　一般人通常會以為山葵泥(Wasabi)具有殺菌之作用，事實上并不然，山葵泥祇是為了增加口感為主要目的。 制作刺身所用的海鮮食材，選購時必須注意新鮮度與肥美，加上由資深料理師出掌，刀工要好、處理與料理、佐料、擺飾的技巧必須非常熟悉與了解，方能制作出一　盤令人在視覺上與味覺上都令人嘖嘖稱贊的刺身料理。目前較常見的刺身種類有：紅魯魯魽、鮭魚、鮪魚、鯛魚(加納魚)、旗魚、龍蝦、蘆蝦等等。其中每年五月份所盛產的黑鮪魚刺身更是令許多食客回味無窮的人間珍品。刺身并不一定都是完全的生食，有些刺身料理也會稍微的經過加熱處理，例如：炭火烘烤：鮪魚腹肉經由炭火略為烘烤，將魚腹油酯經過烘烤而讓其散發出香味，再浸入冰中切片而成。刺身料理通常出現在套餐中或是桌菜，同時也可以作為下酒菜、配菜或是單點的菜色。

137

VII. 日本餐 Japanese Foods

（二）單點品：

傳統式的日本料理，通常以各種不同的烹調方式區分，諸如：油炸類（揚物）、燒烤類（烤物）、炖煮類（煮物）、清蒸（蒸物）、湯類（吸物）以及腌漬小菜等等。油炸類在日本料理菜單上名稱爲[揚物]，或是[炸物]。炸物主要是利用裏上面糊的入炸的食材香又酥，但是內部所包的食材却依然保持滑嫩可口。一般炸物食材有魚、豬肉、蝦、芋頭、蚵、地瓜、茄子、豆腐、青椒、花枝、各類蔬菜及根莖類，隨着料理不斷求新，炸物的種類更加豐富，例如增加了榴槤與牛蒡等。綜合天婦羅（Tempura）在日本料理中就是一道大家耳熟能詳的揚物,主要材料爲白肉魚塊、明蝦，配料爲茄子、青椒、芋頭、地瓜或香菇。

一般揚物料理都會附上已經調味的沾料與白葡萄研末，食用時可將研末放入沾料中調匀，一邊沾一邊吃。常見的炸物，有天婦羅定食、炸蝦、天婦羅、蔬菜天婦羅、炸豬排、炸蚵、炸香菇丸等等。

常見的燒烤方式大略可以分成下列幾種：

1、**素燒**：將沙拉塗抹在食材上，直接于烤箱內烤。

2、**照燒**：將調配好的醬汁一面烤一面塗抹在食材上，直到食物可以食用。

3、**串燒**：將食物串在竹簽上，直接置漁火爐網上，反覆燒烤。

4、**鐵板燒**：將食物置于燒熱的厚鐵板上烹調。

5、**岩燒**：先將石頭或岩石置于火爐上燒烤至300度以上，再將食物，置放在燒熱的岩石上烹調。

6、**姿燒**：以竹簽將整祇魚或是蝦，固定成形，置放於火爐或烤箱內燒烤至熟透。

7、**鹽烤**：以鹽抹遍食材、放入火上、烤箱中燒烤，常見的有鹽烤香魚蝦姑鹽烤等等。

8、味噌烤：將魚類浸入調好的味噌醬內，腌漬數小時後，放置于烤箱內烤熟

（三）壽司：

包含平常常風的手卷、握壽司，花壽司等等。

（四）火鍋類：

平常常見的有涮涮鍋、紙火鍋、猪肉火鍋、牛肉火鍋、海鮮火鍋等等。

（五）套餐類：

簡餐型的定食與正式的套餐等等。

醬料 Sauce

Abalone Flavored Sauce	御品鮑魚汁		
Apple Flavored Vinegar	蘋果醋		
Chili Fermented Bean Curd with Sesame Oil	麻油辣腐乳		
Chili Fermented Bean Curd	辣腐乳		
Crisp Radish	脆蘿卜	Dark Soy Sauce	老抽
Dehydrated Japanese Style Soy Sauce	日式醬油粉		
Delicious Oyster Flavored Sauce	鮮味蚝油		
Fermented Red Bean Curd	南乳/紅腐乳		
Fish Bone and Grilled Meat Sauce	味噌烤肉醬		
Fish Sauce	魚露	Fried Crabs with Soy Sauce	醬油蟹
Fruit Flavored Vinegar	康多果醋	High-grade Light Soy Sauce	高級醬青
Hot Assorted	麻辣什錦	Japanese Barbecue Sauce	和風燒烤汁
Japanese Soya Sauce	龜甲萬醬油		

VII. 日本餐 Japanese Foods

Kikkoman Naturally Brewed Soy Sauce 萬字醬油			
Kikkoman Teriyaki Marinade & Sauce 龜甲萬燒烤醬油			
Light Soy Sauce	生抽	Marinade Sauce	滷水汁
Organic Soy Sauce 有機醬油		Oyster Flavored Sauce	蠔油
Pearl River Oyster Flavored Sauce 珠江蠔油			
Premium Mushroom Soy Sauce		海天特級草菇醬油	
Premium Reduced Salt Soy Sauce		低鹽醬油	
Premium Sweet & Sour Sauce 酸甜汁		Premium Sweet Soy Sauce 甜醬油	
Pure Rice Vinegar 純米醋		Pure Soy Sauce	原汁醬油
Refined Sesame Seed Oil 小磨芝麻油		Rice Vinegar	米醋
Salad Dress 沙律汁醬		Seasoned Soy Sauce for Seafood	蒸魚豉油
Shrimp Flavored Soy Sauce 鮮蝦醬油		Shrimp-Roe Soy Sauce	蝦籽醬油
Soy Sauce	醬油	Superior Soy Sauce	老抽王
Sushi Vinegar	壽司醋		
Springfield Soy Sauce Authentic Seasoning 春田優質大豆醬油			
Teriyaki Marinade, Sukiyaki		御品鮑魚汁	
Tunny Sauce 金槍魚調味醬		Vegetarian Stir-Fly Sauce 健康素食蠔油	
Wasabi Oil	芥末膏	Wasabi Sauce	芥末汁
Wild Bamboo Shoots 野竹笋		Yamasa Sushi Soy Sauce 上字壽司醬	
Yellow Label Soy Sauce 黃標醬油		Yupin Oyster Flavored Sauce 御品蠔油	

沙律 Salad

Avocado Salad	油梨沙律
Baby Scallop and Okura Salad	岩海苔帆立小柱沙律

Caesar Salad in Chicken Breast	鷄肉凱撒色拉		
Caesar Salad	西澤沙律	Chef Salad	廚師沙律
Chicken Salad	鷄肉沙律	Cole Slaw	凉拌生菜絲
Cucumber With Miso Salad	日式醬黃瓜沙律		
Cucumber Salad	青瓜沙律	Daikon Chicken Salad	大根細麵雞絲沙律
Egg Salad	鷄蛋沙律		
Fried Crab Stick on Salad With Ginger Sauce	炸蟹絲沙律佐薑汁醋醬		
Fruit Salad	水果沙律	Garden Salad	田園沙律
Green Salad	青菜沙律	Ham and Cheese Salad	生火腿幹酪卷沙律
Macaroni Salad	通心粉沙律	Pineapple Salad	菠蘿沙律
Potato Salad	薯仔沙律	Rare Grilled Tuna Salad	炙燒鮪魚沙律
Salad / Salad Dressing	沙律 / 沙律醬	Salmon Salad	鮭魚生魚片沙律
Sea Urchin with Vegetable Salad	海膽和風沙律		
Seafood Salad	和風海鮮沙律	Seaweed Salad	海草沙律
Shrimp Salad in Salmon Roe	三文魚籽鮮蝦沙律	Shrimp Salad	蝦沙律
Spinach Salad	菠菜沙律	Thousand Island Dressing	千島沙律醬
Vegetable Salad	什菜沙律		

面類 Noodles

Beef Udon Noodle	牛肉烏冬或蕎麥面	Cold Noodle	日式涼面
Curry Noodle	咖喱烏冬面	Fried Noodle with Kim Chi	泡菜炒烏冬面
Green Tea Flavored Buckwheat Noodle	茶味蕎麥面		
Hot Chili Noodle	激辣拉面	Japanese Style Fried Noodle	日式炒烏冬面
Miso Noodle	醬湯拉面	Mix Vegetable Noodle	蔬菜拉面

VII. 日本餐 Japanese Foods

Pork Soup Noodle	骨湯拉面	Pork Rib Noodle	排骨拉面
Roast Pork Noodle	醬油叉燒面	Seafood Noodle	海鮮烏冬面
Sautéed Noodles With Beef and Green Pimento			鐵板炒烏冬面

天婦羅 Tempura

Deep Fried Carrot	炸蘿卜	Deep Fried Chicken Breast	炸雞塊
Deep Fried Pig Skin with Asparagus	蘆笋脆皮肉	Deep Fried Pork	炸猪排
Deep Fried Spanish Paprika	炸青椒	Deep Fried Vegetables	紫蘇天婦羅
Fried Bean Curd	炸豆腐	Fried Chicken	炸雞肉
Fried Egg	煎蛋	Fried Fishes	油炸物
Fried Flatfish	炸墨魚須	Fried Pork	炸猪排
Fried Pork with Kimchi	和風泡菜炒猪肉	Fried Shrimps	炸蝦排
Fried Tofu	炸豆腐	Fried Vegetable	蔬菜天婦羅
Japanese Style Fried Spinach	日式炒菠菜		
Japanese Style Fried Bitter Herbs	日式炒苦菜		
Vegetable and Pork Roll	菜肉卷天婦羅		

生魚片 Sashimi (Raw Fish)

Ark Shell	赤貝	Bonito	鰹魚
Assorted Sashimi	綜合生魚片	Black Sea Bass	鱸魚
Cod Roe with Chili	雪魚籽	Cold Platters	冷盤（刺身）
Conch	海螺	Conger Eel	星鰻
Crab Meat	蟹肉	Cuttlefish	墨鬥魚

Eel	鰻魚	Flying Fish Roe	三文魚
Fresh Shrimp Appetizer	生鮮蝦片	Giant Clam	象拔蚌
Herring	青魚，鯡	Lobster	龍蝦
Mackerel	青花魚	Mixed Fresh Tunny Meat	生拌金槍魚肉
Octopus	章魚	Oyster	壕
Prawn	明蝦	Red Clam	赤貝
Red Snapper	加吉魚	Salmon Roe	三文魚卵
Salmon	三文魚	Sailfish	鯕魚生魚
Scallop	扇貝	Scallop	柱貝
Sea Bass	黑鱸	Sea Bream	加吉魚
Sea Urchin Roe	海膽	Sea Urchin	海膽
Seafood and Radish	海鮮刺身	Shrimp	蝦
Spanish Mackerel	馬鮫魚	Squid	魷魚,烏賊
Stripped Sea Bass		Surf Clam	北極貝
Sweet Shrimp	甜蝦	Swordfish	箭魚
Trout	鱒魚	Tuna Fatty Meat	金槍魚腩
Tuna	金槍魚	Yellow Tail	黃獅魚

Arctic Pole Shellfish Sashimi 北極貝刺身

Assorted Sashimi Platter 綜合刺身拼盤

Australian Iced Abalone Sashimi 原衹澳洲凍鮑魚

Beef Sashimi	牛肉刺身	Bream & Salmon Sashimi	鯛魚三文魚刺身
Geoduck Sashimi	象拔蚌活造	Live Lobster	龍蝦刺身
Live Flatfish	比目魚活造	Live Lobster Sashimi	大龍蝦刺身

Live Geoduck Sashimi 象拔蚌刺身

Live Leopard Coral Grouper Sashimi 原條大東星斑刺身

Live Tubo Sashimi 原條多寶魚刺身

VII. 日本餐 Japanese Foods

Mackerel & Salmon Sashimi		醋青魚三文魚刺身	
Mixed 6 Sashimi 六拼刺身		Octopus Sashimi	涼制八蛸
Oyster Sashimi 生蚝刺身		Shellfish Sashimi	北極貝刺身
Salmon Sashimi 三文魚刺身		Scallop Sashimi	帶子刺身
Sea Bass Sashimi 鱸魚刺身		Surf Clam Sashimi	北極貝刺身
Tuna & Octopus Sashimi		金槍魚八爪魚刺身	
Tuna & Salmon Sashimi		金槍魚三文魚刺身	
Tuna Sashimi 金槍魚刺身			

燒烤類 Broiled Dishes

Broiled Chicken Leg with Teriyaki Sauce		醬汁烤雞排	
Broiled Codfish 醬烤鱈魚		Broiled Cuttlefish	烤魷魚
Broiled Egg Plant with Condiments		烤茄子	
Broiled Mackerel 鹽烤鯖花魚		Broiled River Eel	烤鰻魚
Grilled Bean Curd 鐵板豆腐		Grilled Chicken	日式烤雞
Grilled Salty Mackerel		鹽燒日本青花魚	
Grilled Head of Yellowtail		烤黃獅魚	
Grilled Sanma with Salt 鹽烤秋刀魚		Grilled Smelts	烤多春魚
Grilled Salmon Head Japanese Style		日式燒三文魚頭	
Grilled Salty Codfish		日式燒多春魚	
Grilled Potato With Milk		土豆奶汁烤菜	
Grilled Salmon Neck 烤三文魚頸		Grilled Salmon Belly	烤三文魚腩
GriLled Saury 烤秋刀魚			

湯 Soups

Agar Thick Soup	羊羹	Clam Meat Soup	蜆肉周打湯
Clams Soup	蛤蜊湯	Clear Soup	清湯
Conger Eel and Chicken Soup		海鰻雞骨湯	
Egg & Vegetable Soup		蛋花湯	
Egg Drop Soup With Mushroom		蘑菇蛋花湯	
Fish Ball Soup	魚丸湯	Fish Bone Soup	味噌湯
Hot & Sour Soup Szechuan Style		四川酸辣湯	
Lobster Bisque	法式龍蝦湯	Meat Ball Soup	貢丸湯
Minced Chicken with Sweet Corn Thick Soup		雞蓉粟米羹	
Miso Soup	味噌湯	Moray Soup	海鰻湯
Oyster Soup	牡蠣湯	Pork Intestine Soup	猪腸湯
Pork Thick Soup	肉羹湯	Prawn Soup	明蝦湯
Sea Scallop of Green Asparagus Soup		蘆笋幹貝奶湯	
Seafood Noodle SOup 海鮮湯麵		Seaweed Soup	紫菜湯
Shrimp Wonton Soup 鮮蝦雲吞湯		Soya Sauce Soup	大醬湯
Spicy Miso Soup	辣味噌湯	Squid Soup	魷魚湯
Squid Thick Soup	花枝羹	Sweet & Sour Soup	酸辣湯
Wonton Soup	餛飩湯		

壽司卷 Sushi Rolls

Anago-Sugata Roll 幹瓢星鰻卷		Asparagus Hand Roll	蘆筍手捲
Assorted Nigiri Platter 綜合握壽司		Assorted Roll Platter	綜合壽司

VII. 日本餐 Japanese Foods

Assorted Sushi Roll 什錦壽司卷		Avocado Roll	牛油果卷
Bean Curd Sheet Sushi 豆腐皮壽司		Big Roll	特制粗卷
Bock Roll	葫蘆卷	California Roll	加州卷
California Hand Rolled 加州手卷		Crab Meat Hand Roll	蟹柳手卷
Cooked Prawn Hand Roll		熟蝦手卷	
Cooked Tuna Hand Roll 熟吞拿魚手卷		Crabstick Sushi	蚧柳壽司
Cucumber & Flying Fish Roe Maki Roll 青瓜飛魚籽小卷			
Cucumber Roll	黃瓜卷	Dragon Roll	火龍酪梨卷
Eel Hand Roll	鰻魚手捲	Eel Roll	鰻魚手卷
Eel Wrapped In Egg Roll		鰻魚鷄蛋卷	
Fermented Soy Beans Rolled in Seaweed			納豆卷
Flower Roll	花壽司	Flying Fish Roe Hand Roll	飛魚籽手卷
Great Burdock Hand Roll		牛蒡絲手捲	
Grilledunagi Hand Roll 鰻魚手捲		Grilled Unagi Hand Roll	鰻魚手捲
Ikura and Smoked Salmon Roll		奶油起司鮭魚親子卷	
Minced Meat Roll 肉鬆壽司卷		Mixed Vegetable Roll	太卷
Pickle Roll	黃咸菜卷		
Roasted Sushi and Duck Meat in Bamboo Slip 燒竹簡及鴨片伴壽司			
Pickled Radish Roll 東京蘿卜壽司卷			
Rainbow Roll	彩虹卷	Raw Tuna with Seasoned Rice	黑鮪壽司
Roll Sushi	卷物	Salmon Hand Roll	三文魚手卷
Salmon Roe Hand Roll		鮭魚卵手捲	
ScalloP, Avocado & Spicy-Mayonnaise Sauce Roll 帆立貝酪梨味噌卷			
Sesame Roll	芝麻壽司卷	Seaweed Roll	海苔壽司
Shimesaba Roll (Preserved) Mackerel Roll 醋漬青花魚卷			
Shrimp Hand Roll 蝦手捲		Shrimp Roe Hand Roll	蝦卵手捲

Shrimp Roll	蝦壽司卷		
Smoked Salmon Rolled in Potato		烟熏三文魚土豆卷	
Spicy Scallop Roll	辣帶子卷	Spicy White Tuna	辣吞拿魚壽司
Spider Roll	蜘蛛軟殼蟹卷	Surf Clam Sushi	北杯貝壽司
Sushi Rice Packaged in Egg Pancake			茶巾壽司
Sushi With Eel	和風星鰻散壽司	Sushi with Plum	梅菜紫菜卷
Taro Roll	芋頭壽司	Tofu Sushi	豆皮壽司
Tuna Hand Roll	金槍魚手卷	TuNa Roll	鐵火捲 (金槍魚壽司捲)
Tuna And Seasoned Rice Rolled in Seaweed			海苔鮪魚細卷
Vegetable Roll	蔬菜壽司卷	Yellow Greek Dace	黃希鯪押壽司

菜單講解 Dishes Explanation

Dragon Roll consists of tempura shrimp, cucumber and avocado.
飛龍卷裏有蝦天婦羅,黃瓜和牛油果。

Rainbow Dragon consists of salmon, tuna and with white tuna on top.
彩虹龍卷有三文魚，金槍魚及白金槍魚在上面。

Sider Roll is a combination of soft shell crab, cucumber and avocado.
軟殼蟹卷有軟殼蟹，黃瓜及牛油果。

Dynamite consists of tempura shrimp, cucumber and avocado.
大蝦天婦羅卷有蝦天婦羅，黃瓜及牛油果。

Sunshine Roll consists of deep fried fish meat with salmon on top plus spicy sauce. 陽光卷有炸魚肉及三文魚和辣醬。

Rain Bowl Roll is a combination of California roll with salmon, tuna and white tuna on top.
彩虹卷由加州卷組成及外面有三文魚和金槍魚。

147

VII. 日本餐 Japanese Foods

Mango Roll consists of crab meat, tempura bits, avocado on top and mango sauce. 芒果卷有蟹肉，碎天婦羅，牛油果在外面及芒果醬油。

Volcano Roll consists of deep fried assorted fish & avocado with spicy sauce. 火山卷有炸雜魚，牛油果及辣醬油。

其它菜單 Other Dishes

Beef Teriyaki	照汁串烤牛肉	Boiled Egg	煮蛋
Boiled Radish Strips	漆匠蘿卜	Braised Beef	炖牛肉
Braised Button Mushroom with Crab Sticks			蟹柳扒鮮草菇
Braised Chop with Kelp	海帶燒排骨		
Braised Pork with Sauce	勝井		
Braised Salmon Belly with Chef's Special Sauce			甘香三文魚頭腩
Broccoli on Ice	冰鎮芥藍	Chef's Special	主廚特餐
Cuttlefish with Codfish Roe	鱈魚籽拌墨魚		
Eggplant and Meat Pie	茄子肉餅		
Fried Bean Sprout with Preserved Vegetable			魚卵小壽
Fried Salted Chicken with Broccoli			芥藍炒咸鷄
Garden Pea Dumplings	荷蘭豆燒麥		
Green Pepper and Meat Pie	青椒肉餅		
Pan Fried Potato Croquette with Vegetable			鐵板土豆餅
Pan Fried Scallops with Butter	香煎牛油帶子		
Pan Fried Shrimps with Butter	香煎牛油蝦		
Pan Fried Squid	香煎牛油魷魚		
Pancake in Meat with Vegetable	風味肉卷單餅		
Potato Crab and Fish Cake	土豆蟹魚糕		

Prawn and Oyster with Flour Sauce	面豉燒龍蝦生豪伴海膽		
Prawns Baked in A Pan	鍋塌明蝦		
Pumpkin with Chicken	南瓜鷄米	Roast Meat	鐵板烤肉
Sautéed Pork Ribs in Chili Sauce	炒辣椒排骨		
Special Salty Crab	秘制咸羔蚧	Seafood Chaffy Dish	海鮮小火鍋
Simmered Dishes	煮菜		
Simmered Kombu-Fish Rolls	煮昆布小魚		
Soy Simmered Golden Thread	煮金綫魚		
Steamed Seafood in Teapot	茶壺蒸海鮮		
Stone Fire Pot	石頭火鍋	Stuffed Tofu Pockets	福袋煮
Sunny Side Up	煎一面荷包蛋	Tai Kabutoyaki	烤加吉魚頭
Teriyaki Chicken	日式照燒雞排	Tomato and Meat Pie	蕃茄肉餅

飯類 Donburi Rice

Assorted Fried Rice Toppan Yaki	鐵板什錦炒飯
Curried Chicken Strips with Rice	鷄排咖喱飯
Fried Crispy Chicken Strips with Rice	脆皮鷄排飯
Pork Cutlet & Egg with Rice	猪排飯
Shrimp Curry with Rice	脆皮蝦咖喱飯
Sautéed Chicken with Rice	照燒鷄蓋飯
Sautéed Beef with Rice	牛肉蓋飯
Sautéed Eel with Rice	鰻魚飯
Sautéed Pork with Rice	猪肉蓋飯
Sirloin Fried Rice Toppan Yaki	鐵板牛肉炒飯

VII. 日本餐　Japanese Foods

套餐 Set Courses

Chicken Steak Set	鐵板鷄肉套餐
Salmon Roe with Salmon on Rice	三文魚紅魚子壽司飯
Shrimp with Vegetables Tempura Sprinkled with Soy-Seasoned Broth	蝦仁蔬菜天婦羅蓋飯
Tempura Selection on Rice Set	天婦羅蓋澆飯套餐
Fried Beef and Rice Set	燒牛肉蓋飯套餐
Deep Fried Pork in Egg on Rice Set	炸猪排蓋飯套餐
Special lunch Box	精制日式餐盒
Grilled Codfish Set	烤銀雪魚套餐
Mini Sukiyaki Set	鷄素燒套餐
Sashimi Set	生魚片套餐
Sushi Set	壽司套餐
Tempura Set	天婦羅套餐
Deep Fried Pork Set	炸猪排套餐
Deep Fried Prawn Set	炸蝦排套餐
Broiled River Eel	鰻魚蓋飯套餐
Deep Fried Pork Shop Over Steamed Rice with Curry Sauce	咖喱猪排飯套餐
Steamed Rice with Curry Flavored	咖喱飯套餐
Grilled Cubed Beef Steak Set	鐵板牛肉套餐
Seafood Steak Set	鐵板海鮮套餐

常用句子 Useful Sentences

Do you need help ordering?	您需要幫忙點菜嗎？
Is the food here good?	這的飯菜好吃嗎？
It's great food at the great prices.	物美價廉。
I'm going to have the sushi and some Miso soup.	我要壽司和味噌湯。
Shall I bring you some wasabi as well?	要我給您拿點青芥末嗎？

English	Chinese
What else do you want?	其他的還要點什麼?
I'll have some sashimi and some teriyaki chicken.	我要一些生魚片和一些紅燒雞塊。
That's a good choice.	明智的選擇。
Do you have sake?	您們有日本米酒嗎?
Do you want a bottle or a glass?	您們要一瓶還是一杯?
So tell me about the food here.	給我講講這的飯菜。
We eat a lot of fresh fish and short-grain rice.	我們吃了許多新鮮的魚還有短粒米。
Have you ever tried it?	您以前吃過嗎?
Do you want to try some?	您想嘗一些嗎?
Taste this.	嘗嘗這個。
Do you like it?	你喜歡嗎?

情景對話 | Situational Dialogue |

W=Waiter 服務生 C=Customer 客人

Waiter: Welcome to Super Top Number One Restaurant. Do you need help ordering?

服務生：歡迎來到超級第一餐廳。您需要幫助點菜嗎?

Customer: No, I lived in Japan a few years ago. Is the food good here?

顧客：不用，我幾年前在日本住過。這的飯菜好吃嗎?

W: Oh, yes. It's great food at great prices.

服務生：當然，物美價廉。

C: OK. I'm going to have the sushi and some miso soup.

顧客：好的。我想來點壽司和一些味噌湯。

W: OK, shall I bring you some wasabi as well?

服務生：好，要我給您拿一些青芥末嗎?

VII. 日本餐 Japanese Foods

C: Yes, please do. 顧客：是的，請。

W: I'll. What else do you want?

服務生：一會兒給你，其他的您還想要什麼？

C: I'll have some sashimi and some teriyaki chicken.

顧客：我想來些生魚片和紅燒雞塊。

W: That is a good choice. 服務生：有眼光。

C: Do you have saki? 顧客：你這有日本米酒嗎？

W: Of course we do. Do you want a bottle or a glass?

服務生：當然有。您要一瓶還是一杯？

C: Bring me a bottle and I'll take it home.

顧客：給我拿一瓶，剩下的我要帶回家去。

W: Certainly. Is that all? 服務生：行，齊了嗎？

C: That's all for now. 顧客：現在已經齊了。

W: OK, I'll be right back with the saki.

服務生：好的，我馬上拿米酒過來。

情景對話 II Situational Dialogue II

W=Waiter 服務生 C=Customer 客人

Customer: So tell me about the food here.

顧客：那請給我講講這的菜吧。

Waiter: Japanese food is the best food in the world. It's very healthy.

服務生：日本餐是世界上最好的。它非常健康。

C: That's good to know. 顧客：了解一下很有幫助。

W: We eat a lot of fresh fish and short-grain rice.

服務生：我們吃很多新鮮的魚，還有短粒米。

C: I heard you eat raw fish, it that true?

顧客：我聽說您們吃生魚，是嗎？

W: Yes it is. Have you ever tried it?　　服務生：是的，您以前吃過嗎？

C: No, should I?　　顧客：没有，我應該嘗試嗎？

W: Oh, yes. I'll bring you some roe.

服務生：哦，是的，我給您拿一些魚卵。

C: What is that?　　顧客：那是什麼？

W: It is raw fish eggs. It is delicious.

服務生：這是生魚子，非常好吃。

C: OK, I'll try it. Do you eat seaweed as well?

顧客：好吧，我嘗嘗這個。 您吃過海藻嗎？

W: Yes, in sushi. Do you want to try some?

服務生：吃過，在壽司裏。您想嘗嘗嗎？

C: Yes, I will.　　顧客：行，我來一些。

W: OK, here you are. Taste this. Do you like it?

服務生： 好的，給您，嘗嘗這個吧，喜歡嗎？

C:　Yes, it is quite nice. But I don't think it's the best food in the world.

顧客： 喜歡，非常好吃，但是我不認爲這是世界上最好的食物。

W: We'll have to agree to disagree.　　服務生：我們各自保留意見吧.

C: No, the customer is always right.

顧客：不，顧客總是對的。

介紹菜單會話 Introducing Dishes Conversation

(W=Waiter 服務生 G=Guest 客人)

W: Good evening. ……Are you ready to order, sir?

晚上好！……先生，您要點什麼？

G: Yes. What kind of food is the tempura?

甜不辣是什麼樣的菜？

153

VII. 日本餐 Japanese Foods

W: It's fish, prawns and assorted vegetables dipped in batter and then deep fried until crisp. It's very popular with both Japanese and foreign guests.
那是用魚、蝦和各種蔬菜沾面糊，然後一直炸到變脆，很受日本人和外國客人的喜愛。

G: Um. It sounds delicious. We'll have the tempura dinner for two, please.
嗯。聽起來好像很美味可口。我們要兩份甜不辣晚餐。

W: The tempura dinner comes with raw fish. Will that be fine?
甜不辣晚餐加生魚片，這樣好不好？

G: I see. Well, I'll take the raw fish but my wife doesn't care for it. Could she have something else instead?
哦。嗯，我吃生魚片，但我太太不喜歡。她能吃點其他的東西來代替嗎？

W: Certainly, sir. I would recommend the "Chawanmushi". It's an egg custard with chicken, shrimp and gingko nuts.
當然可以，先生。我建議點"蒸鷄蛋羹"。那是加鷄肉、小蝦、杏仁蒸的蛋羹。

G: O.K. She'll try that.
好，她就試試看那個。

W: Certainly. Just a moment, please.
好的。請稍待片刻。

VIII. 處理抱怨
Handling Complaints

- ☑ 處理抱怨的常用句型 Key Expressions
- ☑ 情景對話 Situational Conversations
- ☑ 衛生檢查 Sanitary Inspection
- ☑ 店鋪維修 Restaurant Repairs

VIII. 處理抱怨 Handling Complaints

外賣餐館情景對話
Situational Dialogues at Take-out Restaurants

處理抱怨的常用句型
Key Expressions

服務不及時 Delayed Service

How much longer shall I wait for my Peking Roasted Duck?
我點的北京烤鴨還得等多久啊？

I've been trying to catch your attention now for the last 20 minutes.
我在這兒已經等了足足20分鐘了。

This is taking too long.
我們等得太久了。

My meal hasn't come yet. Why is it taking too long?
我的菜還沒有來。怎麼要這麼久呢？

I'm sorry. I'll check your order with the chef. Just a moment please.
對不起，我馬上去廚房看一下，請稍等。

I'm really sorry. Please wait a few more minutes. I'll take it to you as soon as possible. 很抱歉，請多等一會兒。一準備好，我會盡快給您上菜。

Sorry to have kept you waiting. I'll see to it right away.
讓您久等，真抱歉。我馬上去處理。

I'll see about your order, but the Peking Roasted Duck you ordered takes quiet a while to prepare.
我會去看您點的菜怎樣了，但是做北京烤鴨是很費時間的。

I've checked your order. It will be here in a few minutes.
我去看過了，您點的菜很快就來。

I'm sorry, sir. We are short of help today. Would you like to have a drink first? 先生，對不起，我們今天人手少。您是不是先喝點什麼？

Sorry, sir. Please excuse her. We're very busy today.
對不起，先生。請您原諒她，我們今天實在太忙了。

服務中出現錯誤 Mistakes while Serving

I ordered Spaghetti, but got Macaroni!
我點了意大利粉，結果上的是通心粉。

We ordered hot noodles, not cold noodles.
我們點的是熱面條，不是凉面。

We ordered the non-spicy dish, why is it still spicy?
我們點的是不辣的，怎麼拿來的是辣的？

Sorry, I'll change it for you right now. 真抱歉，我馬上去換。

I'll have them prepare another one. 我去給您重新端一份。

I didn't order this fish. 我没有點這道魚。

Let me check it up. Well, there is no mistake, sir. This is the very dish you ordered. 讓我查對一下。先生，這個没有錯，這正是您要點的菜。

Sorry, it's my mistake. I have the wrong table.
對不起，是我弄錯了，我看錯臺號了。

.I'm sorry. I've made a mistake with your dish. Will you please repeat your order? 非常抱歉，搞錯了您的菜。請問您點的是什麼菜？

Excuse me. I seem to have brought you the wrong dish.
不好意思，我好像上錯了一個菜。

We made the reservation yesterday. Would you please check again? I'm sure there must be a mistake.
我們昨天訂了位置，您能否再查查看？一定是你們搞錯了！

157

VIII. 處理抱怨 Handling Complaints

Your table is already available, I checked the wrong name.
您的位置已經訂好了，剛才是我看錯名字了。

You said that it would be about 10 minutes; it has been 15 minutes now. Are we going to have a table now? 您剛才說等10分鐘左右就可以，現在已經超過15分鐘了。有桌子給我們了嗎？

Sorry, I didn't estimate the waiting time right. However, we have now arranged a table for you.
對不起，剛才是我把時間估計錯了。不過我已經幫您安排座位了。

Excuse me. We are still waiting for the knives and forks.
打擾一下。我們要的刀叉怎麼還沒有來？

Here are the knives and forks. Sorry for the wait.
這是您要的刀叉。抱歉讓您久等了。

The bill is more than I thought. Can you explain it?
結的賬比我預想的多，您能解釋一下嗎？

I'm afraid you've overcharged me. 恐怕您多算了我的費用。

You may check the bill if you think there is something wrong in it.
您認為有什麼錯誤的話可以再仔細核對一下。

We didn't order stewed fish head, why is it on the bill?
我們沒有點紅燒魚頭，賬單上怎麼會有這個呢？

Sorry, I'll ask the cashier to check it again.
很抱歉，我讓收銀員給您再算算看。

I want the invoice, not the receipt. 我要的是發票，不是收據。

Sorry, I would get the invoice for you in a minute.
抱歉，我們馬上把發票給您。

I'm awfully sorry to stain your suit. I'll bring a cloth for you immediately.
非常抱歉把您的衣服弄髒了，我馬上為您拿布來。

We'll arrange for your suit to be cleaned at once.

我馬上安排將您的西裝拿去清洗。

抱怨菜肴/酒水/餐具質量差 Complaining Dishes/Drinks/Tableware

The meat is underdone / overdone! 這份牛排還未熟/太老了!

The meat is raw/bloody! 這份牛排半生不熟/還有血水!

The meat is too tough/hard! 這份牛排嚼不爛/太硬!

The meat is too dry! 這份牛排太乾澀!

This soup is cold/lukewarm. 這湯是冷的/不夠熱。

This soup is tepid/tasteless. 這湯是微溫的/味道太淡。

This soup is flavorless. 這湯是沒有香味。

This salad is too oily/not fresh. 這個色拉太油膩/不新鮮。

This food tastes strange/funny! 這道菜嘗起來味道很怪/不對勁!

This food tastes awful/bad! 這道菜嘗起來味道很糟糕/很差!

This toast is too stale/soggy/damp! 這吐司烤得不新鮮/沒烤熟/沒烘透。

This toast is too dark/too light! 這吐司烤得太焦/烤得不夠。

This tea is too strong/ weak! 這茶太濃/淡!

The chicken was overdone. It was as tough as leather. I'd like a discount.
這雞肉太老,咬起來像啃皮革。我要打個折扣。

This perch tastes as if were caught a year ago.
這條鱸魚吃起來好像是一年前撈的。

This glass/bowl/plate is cracked. 這個杯子/碗/碟子有裂縫。

This beer is flat! 這個啤酒走味了。

This wine tastes sour/ vinegary! 這酒嘗起來是酸的!

This milk is off/ sour! 這牛奶是酸的!

This cream is rancid. 這個牛奶已經酸臭了。

159

VIII. 處理抱怨 Handling Complaints

There's a (an) hair/insect in my salad! 我的色拉裏有一根頭發/昆蟲。

I'm sorry; I'll change it for you immediately.
對不起，我馬上爲您免費換一份。

I'm very sorry, sir. I'll return your Beef steak to the chef and have them cooked again.
非常對不起，我會把您點的牛排退回廚房再做一份。

If it really bothers you, I'll replace it for you.
如果您覺得這菜確實不合您的意，我可以給你拿去換。

I'll have them prepare another one. Would you like some salad while you are waiting? 我去讓他們再做一份。您要不要先吃點色拉？

Would you like to have a new one or change to another dish?
請問是爲您從做一道菜還是換一份其它菜式呢？

It's complimentary/on the house. 這是本店免費奉送的。

It is free of charge. It's compliments of our restaurant. Enjoy your dinner.
這是不收費的，由我們餐廳免費贈送，請慢用。

對服務態度的抱怨 Complaining Service Attitudes

You've been ignoring us all the evening. We've finished our dinner 20 minutes ago. okey If you don't bring the bill in the next two minutes, we'll leave. 您一整晚都把我們忽視了。我們20分鐘以前就吃完了。如果您不馬上把賬單送來，我們就馬上走。

I'm terribly sorry, sir. We are short of help today.
真抱歉，今天我們人手不足。

I'm very unhappy with your restaurant service. I was badly treated by a rude waiter. He will ruin the reputation of your restaurant. 我對您們餐廳的服務非常地不滿意。 您們的一個服務員態度非常惡劣，他會毀了您們餐廳的聲譽。

I'm terribly sorry about this, sir. Thank you for bring the matter to our attention. I'll look into it. 聽您這樣說我真感到很遺憾。 謝謝您向我們提出問題，我會調查這件事情的。

表示歉意，關注，表達謝意 Apology, Attention, Gratitude

I'm terribly sorry to hear that. 聽到這樣的事情，我真是非常遺憾。

I'll take care of this right away. 我馬上來處理這件事。

I'll look into this matter at once. 我馬上去查清這件事。

We might have overlooked some points.
我們可能忽略了一些細小的地方。

We do apologize for the inconvenience.
我們爲給您帶來的不便深表歉意。

There could have been some mistakes. I do apologize.
可能是出了什麼差錯，實在是對不起。

I'm sorry to hear that. This is quite unusual. I'll look into the matter at once. 我對此很抱歉，這是很少見的，我會馬上調查這件事。

Is there anything wrong with our meal, sir?
您點的菜有什麼問題嗎，先生？

Please accept our apology. 請接受我們的道歉。

I'm terribly sorry, is there anything I can do?
太抱歉了，我能做點什麼嗎？

To express our regret for all the trouble, we offer you a 10% discount and complimentary dessert. 我們給您帶來了這麼多麻煩，爲了表達歉意，特爲您提供9折和免費甜點。

Thank you for telling us sir. I assure you it won't happen again. 感謝您告訴我們，先生。請您放心，這樣的事不會再發生。

VIII. 處理抱怨 Handling Complaints

Thank you for telling us. I'll speak to our manager about it. Please accept our apology.
感謝您告訴我們。我會向經理報告此事,請接受我們的道歉。

I'm terribly sorry. There could have been a mistake. I do apologize.
非常抱歉,一定是出了差錯。

This is really the least we can do for you.
我們能爲您做的實在是太有限了。

Our manager is not in town. Shall I get our assistant manager for you?
我們的經理不在本地。我幫您叫我們的助理經理來好嗎?

I will speak to our manager about it. 我會向我們經理報告這件事情。

Please feel free to contact us if you have any request.
有什麼事情或請求,請即與我們聯絡,不必客氣。

情景對話 Situational Conversations

1. 處理怨言 Handling Complaints

Guest: Waiter! 客人:服務員!

Waiter: Yes. Is there anything wrong with your order, sir?
服務員:來了,您點的菜有什麼問題嗎,先生?

Guest: I'm afraid there is. I just can't understand why this chicken tastes so strange.
客人:恐怕有問題。我不明白爲什麼這鷄肉吃上去味道這麼怪。

Waiter: Pardon me, sir. But didn't you order the Braised Spring Chicken in Butter? 服務員:對不起,先生。您不是點的黃油燜子鷄嗎?

Guest: Sure, I did. Is that what it is?
客人:當然是了。難道就是這個?

Waiter: I think so. But if it really bothers you, I'll replace it for you.

服務員：我想是的。不過如果您覺得這菜確實不合您口味，我可以給您拿去換。

Guest: No, don't replace it. Give me a refund. 客人：別換了。退錢吧。

Waiter: Sorry, we don't refund money, but you may order something else instead.

服務員：對不起，我們不退錢，但您可以另點一道菜來代替。

Guest: Oh, really? That is good. Then give me a Fried Spring Chicken.

客人：哦，真的嗎？很好。那麼就給我一份炸子雞吧。

Waiter: Certainly, sir. Just a moment, please.

服務員：當然可以，先生。請稍候。

2. 對食物的怨言 Complaining Foods

Waiter: Is everything to your satisfaction?

服務員：一切還合您的意嗎？

Guest: No, the steak was recommended, but it is not very fresh.

客人：不合意。您們推薦的牛排不是很新鮮。

Waiter: Oh! Sorry to hear that! This is quite unusual as we have fresh steak from the market every day! I'll look into the matter.

服務員：哦？真遺憾！這是很少發生的，因為我們的牛肉是每天從市場買來的新鮮牛肉。我會調查這件事的。

Guest: So what? It is not fresh and I'm not happy about it!

客人：那又怎樣？牛排不新鮮，我很不滿意！

Waiter: I'm sorry, sir. Do you wish to try something else? That would be on the house, of course. How about a delicious dessert, with our compliments？

服務員：很抱歉，先生。您是否想吃點別的什麼？由本店請客。一份甜品吧，以表我們的歉意，怎樣？

163

VIII. 處理抱怨 Handling Complaints

Guest: No, I don't want to try something else, and find it's not fresh again! This is very annoying.

客人：不必了。我不想再要什麼，否則發現又不新鮮。真讓人惱火！

Waiter: I see, sir. Just give us another chance, you will find this restaurant really lives up to its name. I'm sure everything will be all right next time you come.

服務員：我明白您的心情。請再給我們一次機會，您會發現我們餐廳是名副其實的。我保證您下次來的時候一切都會很好的。

Guest: All right. Maybe I'll come again. 客人： 好的，我下次再來吧。

Waiter: Thank you very much, sir. 服務員：謝謝您的理解，先生。

3. 上菜太慢 Service is Slow

對話 I Dialogue I

Guest: Waiter, I order my meal at least twenty minutes ago and it hasn't come yet. Why is taking so long?

客人：服務員，我已經點餐至少有二十分鐘了，到現在都還沒上菜，爲什麼這麼久的？

Waitress: I'm very sorry, sir. I'll check your order with chef.

女服務員：非常抱歉，先生。我去廚師那裏跟進一下你點的菜。

Guest: Please do and hurry up! I've got to rush to a meeting.

客人：請快點。我得趕去開會。

Waitress: Just a moment, please.

女服務員：請稍候。

Waitress: Your meal, sir. I'm very sorry for the delay. Please enjoy your meal. 女服務員：您的飯菜來了，先生。非常抱歉耽誤了您的時間。請慢用。

對話 II Dialogue II

Diner: Waiter! 就餐者：服務生！

Waiter: Yes, Sir? 服務生：先生，您有什麼事嗎？

Diner: I've been trying to catch your attention now for the last 20 minutes!

就餐者：我在這兒已經等了足足20分鐘了！

Waiter: I'm sorry, sir. I will check it for you right now.

服務生：先生，太抱歉了，我馬上去看看。

Diner: How much longer we're going to have to wait for our dinner?

就餐者：為了這頓晚餐，我們還得等多長的時間？

Waiter: I'm afraid the Peking Roasted Duck takes quite a while to prepare. I'll see about your order. Would you like a salad while you're waiting?

服務生：您要的北京烤鴨恐怕還要等一會兒，我再去看看您點的菜。這段時間您要不要來份色拉？

Diner: No, thanks. 就餐者：不必了。

4.出錯菜或拿錯菜 Served Wrong Dishes

Waitress: Here is the Grilled Beef Steak.

女服務員：這是您點的鐵扒牛排。

Guest: Grilled Beef Steak? I'm afraid you are mistaken.

客人：鐵扒牛排？恐怕你弄錯了。

Waitress: Let me check. Well, there is no mistake. This is the very dish you order.

女服務員：讓我查對一下。這個，沒有弄錯，這正是您點的菜。

Guest: But…Well, to be frank, I don't really care for it. Can I have it changed?

客人：但是…這個，實話實說，我不太喜歡這個菜。能換一換嗎？

VIII. 處理抱怨 Handling Complaints

Waitress: I'm afraid not. Once it is served, it is served.

女服務員：恐怕不能。菜上了就不能換了。

Guest: That is all right. 客人：那就算了。

5. 餐具 Tableware

Guest: Waitress! 客人：服務員

Waitress: Yes, sir! 女服務員：來了，先生！

Guest: Look, these two plates have spots on them!

客人：瞧，這兩個盤子上有點污點！

Waitress: I'm very sorry sir. I'll replace them right away.

女服務員：真對不起，先生。我馬上拿去換。

Guest: And this glass is cracked.

客人：這衹玻璃杯有裂痕。

Waitress: I'm awfully sorry, sir. I'll change it for you right now.

女服務員：實在對不起，先生。我馬上給您換一衹。

Waitress: Here are the brand-new plates and glass, sir. I'm very sorry for my carelessness. 女服務員：這是嶄新的盤子和杯子，先生。非常抱歉，剛才我太粗心了。

Guest: That is all right. 客人：沒關系。

6. 意外事件 Accident

Guest: Look what you've done! You spilled on my shirt!

客人：看看您幹的好事！您把湯濺到我襯衣上了。

Waitress: I'm awfully sorry to have stained your shirt. I'll bring you a cloth immediately.

女服務員：非常抱歉把您的襯衣給弄臟了。我馬上拿塊布來。

Guest: Yes, be quick. 客人：好，快點。

Waitress: I'd like to apologize for my carelessness. May I clean it up for you? 女服務員：我爲我們的粗心大意向您表示歉意。我可以替您擦幹净嗎？

Guest: No, I'll do it myself. 客人：不用了，我自己來。

Waitress: Are you a hotel guest? 女服務員：你是住在酒店的客人嗎？

Guest: No, and what's got to do with it?

客人：不是。那有什麽關系嗎？

Waitress: Here is my card, sir. Could you send us the cleaning bill and we will refund the dry cleaning cost to you?
女服務員：先生，這是我的名片。請把洗衣賬單寄給我們，我們會把錢退給您的，好嗎？

Guest: I should think so, too. 客人：我想也該如此。

Waitress: I'm sorry to have caused you any trouble.
女服務員：很抱歉給您帶來這種麻煩。

Guest: Please be more careful in the future. 客人：今後要當心點。

Waitress: I will sir. I'm really very sorry.
女服務員：我會的，先生。真的很對不起。

Guest: That's OK. 客人：算了。

衛生檢查
Sanitary Inspection

衛生局官員 Inspection Officer　　餐館經理 Manager

Inspection Officer：This morning someone called to complain that after eating your General Tsao's Chicken. He became ill. 衛生局官員：上午有個客人打電話抱怨，吃了你餐館做的佐宗鷄之後，病了。

167

VIII. 處理抱怨 Handling Complaints

Manager: In all the years we've been doing business here, no one has ever complained, nor has any customer ever become ill after eating our dishes. If you don't believe me, you can check to see if the food in the refrigerator is contaminated, un-fresh, past the date of expiration or exhibits any other sanitation problem. Obviously, this customer's illness was not caused by our food. 餐館經理：我們餐館開了這麼多年，從來沒有客人抱怨過。也沒有發現客人吃了食物之後得病的問題，不相信你可以查一查我們冰箱內的食物是否變質或不新鮮，是否有保存不妥的地方或其它不衛生的問題。顯然，那位客人不是因為我們的食物而得病。

Inspection Officer: The cooking range is covered with grease and the utensils are dirty. This is unsanitary.
衛生局官員：爐竈附近很油膩，而且器具很髒，不衛生。

Manager: Every day after work we clean the cooking range. As for the wall above, the floor beneath, and the stovetop, we usually clean them every three or four weeks. Tomorrow is Sunday, our cleaning day. Some of the utensils are old and look dirty, but they're actually clean. 餐館經理：我們每天收工時有清潔爐竈。至于爐竈附近的墻壁、爐竈底部的地面以及爐頂，我們一般是三、四個星清潔一次，明天是星期日，就是我們要清潔的時間。有些器具是舊了些，看起來很髒，其實不然。

Inspection Officer： The customer who just called wanted me to come over because he found a cockroach in his food. 衛生局官員： 剛才那位客人打電話要我過來，因為在他的食物裏發現一祇蟑螂。

Manager: Oh. I'm terribly sorry about that。 I'll refund him double the price he paid for the dish. This has never happened here before. As you can see, our restaurant is clean and sanitary - there's not a cockroach in the place. The cockroach could have come in with the order delivered earlier. I guarantee this won't happen again.

餐館經理：哦，非常對不起發生了這種事。我願意以雙倍的金額退回客人的錢。我們從來沒有發現過這種事，你看我們餐館這麼清潔，這麼衛生，根本沒有一衹蟑螂，可能是我們訂購原料時，比如說這衹蟑螂在……裏面。但是我保證這種事情再也不會發生。

Officer: There are cigarette butts in the wastebasket in your kitchen, indicating that your worker(s) have been smoking.

衛生局官員：在你廚房垃圾桶裏有烟蒂，這説明員工在廚房内抽烟。

Manager: I realize that smoking in the kitchen is against regulations. Two of our workers smoke, but they know to smoke outside of the kitchen. They've just disposed of the butts in the wastebasket here.

餐館經理：我知道在廚房抽畑是違法的。實際上，我們這裏有一兩個員工會抽畑，但是他們都很自覺地到廚房之外抽。衹不過把畑蒂扔進這裏垃圾桶而已。

Officer: Why hasn't the cooked rice (brown rice) been placed in the refrigerator?

衛生局官員： 你爲什麽没有把煮好的米飯 (指Brown Rice) 放進冰箱内？

169

VIII. 處理抱怨 Handling Complaints

Manager: Because this rice has just been cooked and it's still hot. If we put it into the refrigerator immediately, it will sour. We're allowing it to cool for a while before refrigerating it.

餐館經理：因為這飯剛煮好，太熱，如果一下子放進冰箱會發酸的，所以我讓它冷一會兒再放進冰箱。

Officer: Why is there unprocessed food on the floor?

衛生局官員：你為什麼把未加工過的食物放在地上？

Manager: We realize that all food products must be stored on shelves which are at least four inches off the floor. We've just been delivered and this is our busiest time of the day - we've haven't yet been able to organize them. We'll do it right now.

餐館經理：我們知道在存放食物時，下面都用架子墊高四英寸，因為這些食物是剛剛送到，現在又是繁忙時間，我們不能及時把它們整理好，現在我們馬上去做。

Officer: A lot of these cans of food have swollen or have been dented. Do you know what to do with them?

衛生局官員：這裏有很多罐頭食品的鐵罐漲起來，有的被壓扁了，你知道要怎樣處理？

Manager: Yes. The food products in the swollen cans have probably gone bad. Cans which have been dented may have small holes which have allowed the air in, contaminating the food. We'll either return these cans to the supplier or we'll dispose of them properly.

餐館經理：知道，漲起來的鐵罐，裏面的食物可能變質，被壓扁的罐頭，可能出現小孔，進入空氣，而使食物變質。我們都會把這些貨物退回原公司，或索性扔掉不用。

Officer: Your menu states that you don't use MSG. Why do you have MSG here? 衛生局官員：你的菜單上寫明不用味精，為什麼這裏還放着味精？

Manager: Our cooks use it every day in preparing their own food, so it's placed with the salt, sugar and other spices. The containers are marked clearly so we won't mix them up.

餐館經理：這些味精是我們員工自己用的，因為我們每天都要用，所以也把它與這些鹽、糖等調味料放在一起，而且我們會都辨別，這是什麼，那是什麼，不會出錯的。

店鋪維修
Restaurant Repairs

冰櫃出問題 Freezer Problems

Receptionist: GW Heating and Cooling Center. May I help you?

接待員：國偉冷暖氣維修中心，我可以幫你嗎？

Store Manager: Yes. We've a problem with our freezer. Will you able to fix it for us?

店經理：是的，我們的冰櫃出了問題，你們能維修嗎？

Receptionist: What's the problem?　什麼問題？

171

VIII. 處理抱怨 Handling Complaints

Store Manager: The freezer's temperature is very unstable. Sometimes, it is too high and sometimes it is too low. Besides, the exterior thermometer is not accurate either. Also, the motor on top of the freezer sounds strange too.
店經理: 冰櫃得溫度非常不穩定,凍櫃的溫度有時太高,有時太低;還有外面的濕度表也不準確,在冷凍箱上的馬達聽起來也有點奇怪。

Receptionist: How urgent are you? We won't have a repairman available until 3pm and he'll probably get to your place by 3:30PM. Is that OK?
接待員: 您們急嗎?我們要到下午3點才有修理員,他可能在下午3點30分左右才可以到達您那裏。這樣可以嗎?

Store Manager: Well, we need to have it fixes as soon as possible because we just received a shipment yesterday. I'm afraid that they will be spoiled.
店經理: 那麼,我們需要盡快把它修好因為昨天我們剛剛進了一批貨;我恐怕他們會變壞。

Receptionist: OK. I'll try my best to make arrangement. Can I have your name, phone number and address, please?
接待員: 可以。我會盡量安排。可以給我您的姓名,電話和地址嗎?

Store Manager: My name is Peter Wang, phone number is 646-688-5622 and address is 888 Flushing Avenue.
店經理: 我的名字是王皮特,電話號碼是 646-688-562地址是法拉盛大道888號。

Receptionist: OK. A plumber should be there in about one hour.
接待員: 好的,維修員大概1小時候就可以到。

Store Manager: Thanks very much. 店經理：非常感謝。

One hour later （一小時後）

Plumber: I am Jackson from GW Heating and cooling center. I am here to fix your freezer.
修理員：我是來自國偉冷暖中心的杰森。我是來修理您們的冰櫃的。

Store Manager: Great. This way, please. 店經理：太好了。請這邊走。

Plumber: You put too much stuff on top of the freezer. The freezer can't get enough ventilation so it overheats. As a result, the motor doesn't work correctly and there isn't enough coolant. I'm going to add some now. Also, the air pump inside the freezer is broken. I'll need to replace it with a new one. 修理員：你放太多東西在冷凍箱上面。所以馬達通風不良，過熱，結果馬達運作不正常，而且雪種也不夠了，我要加一點進去。還有，冰櫃內的風扇已經壞了。我要把它換好。

Store Manager: Oh, I see. 店經理：哦，是這樣嗎？我懂了。

Plumber: We will need to buy a new air pump. Do you want to me buy it for you? 修理員：我們需要買一個新的風扇。您需要我幫您買嗎？

Store Manager: Sure, please. 店經理：當然要，請。

Plumber: I bought this part for $25. Here's the receipt. And my labor is $40 per hour. That works out to $60. So you just give me $85.

173

VIII. 處理抱怨 Handling Complaints

修理員：我買了這些零件 $25。這是發票，我的工錢是每小時 $40，這樣，總共 $60。那麼你要給我 $85。

Store Manager: No problem, but can you guarantee that the freezer will be free of problems for a year or some other period of time?
店經理: 沒問題，但是你能保證這冷凍箱在一年或其它一段時間內不會出什麼問題嗎？

Plumber: Usually. We guarantee our work for half a year. During this period, we'll fix any problem free of charge. 修理員：通常我們保修半年時間。在這時間之內出了問題，我們會免費修理。

Store Manager: Great. Thank you very much.
店經理: 太好了。非常感謝。

Plumber: You're welcome. 修理員：不用謝。

下水道堵塞，水管漏水 Sewer and Drain Problems

Recording machine: This is NY Sewer and Drain Cleaning. Our business hour is 8AM to 7PM Monday to Saturday. Please leave your name, phone number and a brief message after the beep. We will call you back as soon as possible.
電話錄音：這裏是紐約下水道，水管清理服務部。我們的上班時間是星期一到星期六的早上八點到下午七點。請"嘀"一聲後留下你的名字、電話,號碼和留言，我會盡快回給你電話。

Store Manager: My name is Alice and I'm calling from the Chinese Restaurant at 70 Main Street in Allentown. My phone number is 646-688-5622; we got a problem with the Sewer and Drain. Could you please call me back tomorrow morning after 11 0'clock? Thank you.

店經理：我是愛麗絲，由啊倫鎮緬街70號中國餐館打來的。我們餐館的下水道和水管出了問題。明天早上十一點後可以打電話給我嗎？我的電話號碼是646-688-5622。謝謝。

(Next morning 11: 30)（第二天早上十一點半）。

Plumber: May I speak to Alice, Please? 修理員：請叫愛麗絲小姐好嗎？

Store Manager: Yes, speaking. 店經理：是的，我就是。

Plumber: This is Michael from NY Sewer and Drain Cleaning Service. I'm returning your call. 修理員：這是米高由紐約下水道水管清理部門打來的。我回你的電話。

Store Manager: Oh, yes. 店經理：哦，對。

Plumber: What's the problem with the sewer and drain?
修理員：下水道和水管出了什麼毛病？

Store Manager: The sewer is clogged. Sometimes the water backs up and one water pipe is leaking. 店經理：下水道塞住了，有時水倒流出來，而且一個水管漏水。

Plumber: Oh, I see. I'll be over there in thirty minutes.
修理員：哦，我明白了，半小時後我就到那裏。

(Plumber is working)（水管工人正在工作）

175

VIII. 處理抱怨 Handling Complaints

Plumber: The grease trap in the basement is full so the water inside the drain can't go through. That's why the water is backed up. You have to clear the grease trap frequently. Especially during the winter and put a strainer on all water receptacles. Such as sinks, floors, stoves, etc. Now, I'll use this snake to unclog the drain and then I'll pour hot water in to allow the grease to go through easily. This U water pipe joint is loose. I'll fix it with cement.
修理員：在地下室的污水槽已經滿了。所以管道中的水通不下去。這就是水倒流的原因。你必須經常清潔污油箱，特別在這冬天。而且要在流水處裝上過濾器，比如：水槽、地面上、爐頭（邊的水溝）等等。現在，我用這蛇形疏通管器通這些管道，再灌進熱水，使污油容易通。這條U形水管的接頭處鬆了，我要用膠水把它穩固一下。

(Two hours later, everything is fine)（兩個小時後，一切修好了）。

Plumber: Well, we'll charge you $85. 修理員：好，我們收你$85。

Store Manager: How did you come to that figure? 店經理：你是怎樣算的？

Plumber: Our minimum first hour is $50 and then we charge $35 for each additional hour. 修理員：我們最低收費是一個小時，這一小時是 $50，然後每個小時按$35算。

Store Manager: Really? 店經理：是這樣的嗎？

Plumber: Yes. 修理員：是的。

Store Manager: Can you make it a little bit cheaper if I pay you in cash? I don't need a receipt anyway. 店經理：如果我付現金，是否能便宜一點？反正我不需要收據。

Plumber: OK. We'll cut it down $10 to $75.
修理員：可以，那麼減掉 $10，就是 $75。

Store Manager: Thank you very much. 店經理：謝謝你。

Plumber：You're welcome. 修理員：不用謝。

IX. 餐館常用詞
Useful Words for Restaurants

IX. 餐館常用詞 Useful Words

餐館常用詞 Useful Words for Restaurants

3-way intersections	三交路口	Above	之上
Accept	接受（小費）	Add	加
Address	地址	Advance	預先
Agreement	合約、同意	Air conditioning	空調
Alcohol	酒精	Alley	小徑、狹路
Allow	允許	Along	沿着
Amount	總額	And	和、與
Ant	螞蟻		
Apartment	公寓、柏文		
Appetizer	餐前小食（尤指炸食物）		
Apple pie	蘋果餡餅	Around	附近、周圍
Arrive	達到	Available	有空的
Avenue (Ave)	大道	Average income	平均收入
Awful	極糟的	Back	背後
Back up	後備，倒退	Bacteria	細菌
Bake	烤（面包等）	Bank	銀行
Bankbook	存折	Bar	抬，酒吧
Barbecue (BBQ)	烤（排骨、牛肉串等）	Barber shop	理發店
Bartender	酒保、酒吧侍者	Basement	地下室
B-B-Q	烤（排骨等）	Be taken	被訂了
Beach	海灘	Beauty shop	美客廊
Beep	按門鈴（喇叭等）	Begin with	以……開始
Behind	在……後面	Bell	鈴、鐘
Below	之下	Between	在……之間

English	Chinese	English	Chinese
Bitter	苦的	Black	黑的
Bleach	漂白水（粉）	Block	堵住
Block	街區	Bloody	有血水的
Blow	按（汽車）喇叭	Blunt	鈍的
Boil	煮	Boiled	煮的
Bone	骨頭	Boneless	無骨的
Booked up	訂滿了	Boulevard (Blvd)	大街、林蔭大道
Bounce	退票	Braise	以慢火燒、煮
Breakfast	早餐	Brick	磚
Bridge	橋	Broil	燒烤；烤肉
Broken	裂開，斷了，壞了	Brown	棕色的
Buddhist	佛教的	Buffet	自助餐
Bug	蟲	Building	大樓、建築物
Bullet proof glass	防彈玻璃	Burger	漢堡包
Burnt	燒焦的	Busboy	男企臺助手
Busgirl	女企臺助手	Business account	商業戶口
Business zone	商業區	Busy street	熱鬧街
Button	底、底部	Buzz	按門鈴
Cantonese	廣東式，廣東話	Captain	領班
Care	照料，處理	Cash	現金
Cashier	收銀員	Casserole (in pot)	煲
Ceiling	天花板	Ceiling tile	天花板
Cement	水泥、粘合劑	Center	中間、中央
Ceramic tile	瓷磚	Certificate	牌照
Chafing dish	火鍋	Chance	機會
Change	零錢，找頭	Character	漢字

IX. 餐館常用詞 Useful Words

Charge	索價	Cheap	便宜
Check	檢查	Checking account	支票戶口
Cheese	乳酪（芝士）	Chef	廚師
Chemical	化學品	Chinese food	中國菜
Chip	裂開	Choice	選擇
Choose	選擇（動詞）	Chop	切綱、剁碎
Chopped	切細的	Chosen	選擇
Chunk	塊狀	Circle	圈，灣道
City	城市	Clean	把……弄幹净
Clog	堵住	Closed	關門的
Close	近的、接近	Cloth	布
Coat check	衣帽間	Coat rack	衣帽架
Cockroach	蟑螂	Cocktail sauce (hot)	雞尾辣醬
Cold	冷的	Cole slaw	雜菜色拉
College	學院、大學	Combination	組合，混合
Combine	混合	Commercial zone	商業區
Commission	傭金、介紹費	Company	公司
Condo	共有公寓	Consist of	由……構成
Container	容器	Contract	合同
Cook	烹調、廚師	Cool down	冷却
Co-op	合作公寓	Cord	露綫
Corner	拐角、街角	Corporation	有限公司
Counter	櫃臺	Country	國家
County	郡（縣）	Coupon	優惠券
Court	法庭	Court (Ct)	短街、巷、法庭
Crack	裂口	Credit	記帳

Crispy	（炸得）蘇的、脆的	Crispy	酥脆的
Cross	越過、橫過	Cross - street	對面（街）
Crossway	十字路口	Crowd	擁擠
Customer	顧客	Cut	割傷口，切
Cute	可愛	Damage	損壞
Danger	危險	Dash	一橫
Daycare	托兒所	Decorate (decoration)	裝修，裝潢
Deep - fry	炸（成酥脆的）	Degree	度數
Deli	熟食店	Delicacy	佳肴
Delicious	美味的	Delight	令人高興（的東西）
Deliver	送餐（動詞）	Delivery	送餐
Dent	凹進去的	Department of Health	衛生局
Deposit	存錢、壓金	Dessert	餐後甜點
Dice	切粒	Diced	切粒的
Diet	節食	Dine	用餐
Dinner	晚餐	Direct	指示方向
Direction	方向	Dirty	臟的
Discard	掉弃	Discount	折扣
Doggy	狗的	Door lamp	門燈
Double	雙倍的	Down	下
Downtown	下城	Dragon	龍
Drain	排（污）水管，流掉、幹	Drive (Dr)	車道
Driveway	汽車道	Drop	丟
Drug store	藥店	Dust	灰塵
East (E)	東	Eat in	堂吃

IX. 餐館常用詞 Useful Words

Economic depression	經濟蕭條	Electrician	裝電工人
Electricity	電	Empty	空的
End	盡頭、末端	Entree	前菜
Equipment	設備	Especially	特別，尤其
Except	除之外	Exchange	換
Exhaust	抽氣系統	Expect	期待
Expensive	昂貴	Expiration	期限
Express way	高速公路	Exterminator	專業殺蟲人員
Extra	多，額外的	Extra hot	額外辣的
Facile	設備	Factory	工廠
Fahrenheit (F)	華氏度	Family	家庭
Fan	風扇	Fantail	凰尾，形的
Far	速的	Fatty	多脂肪的
Faucet	水龍頭	Fault	過錯
Fine	罰款	Finger	手指
Fire extinguisher	滅火器	Fire prevention system	防火系統
Fix	修理	Flavor	風味
Floor tile	地磚	Flow	溢出來
Fly	蒼蠅	Fly stick	粘蒼蠅膠帶
Foil	箔紙	Follow	接下來
Food	食物	Forgot	忘記了
Fortune	幸運	Free	免費
Fresh	新鮮的	Fried	炸的
Fried	炸的、炒的	From	從
From	從…到…	Front	在……前面
Frozen	急凍	Fry	炒（飯等）、炸

English	Chinese	English	Chinese
Fryer	油爐	Fuse	保險絲
Garage	車房	Gas	煤氣
Gas - station	汽油站	Gas range	爐霹
General	將軍	Get	達到、得到
Gloomy	陰暗	Glove	手套
Go	走、去	Go ahead	向前
Going	繼續走、去	Gourmet	美食家
Grand opening	開業	Grease	油膩
Grease Lap (box)	裝污水雜物的容器（箱）	Greasy	油膩的
Greasy	油膩的	Grocery	雜貨店
Ground	剁碎的	Guarantee	保證
Guest	客人、貴賓	Hair	頭髮
Half	一半	Ham	火腿
Happy	高興	Hard	困難
Hard	硬的	Hawaii	夏威夷
Head waitress	女領班	Hearing	上庭
Heater	加熱器	Here	這裏
Highway	高速公路	Home	家，特有的
Hope	希望	Horn	喇叭
Hospital	醫院	Host	主人、東道主
Hostess	女主人、女侍	Hot	辣的，熱的
Hot dog	熱狗	Hotel	旅館、賓館
House	房子，本樓	House	房子
Humid	潮濕的	I.D	身份
Illegal	不合法	Immediately	馬上
In	在…裏面	Inch	英寸

IX. 餐館常用詞 Useful Words

Include	包括	Income	收入
Industrial zone	工業區	Infection	傳染
Inflammation	發炎	Inn	客棧、旅館
Insect	昆蟲	Inspect	檢查
Install (installation)	安裝	Instead of	代替
Intersection	交叉點、十字路口	Intonation	數據、詢問處
Jell	果凍	Jelly	果凍
Juicy	多汁的	Jumbo	大的
Keep	保持	Kept	保持 (過去式)
Killer	殺蟲藥（器）	Kitchen	廚房
Knock	敲門	L (large)	大的（份量）
Label	標籤	Landlord	房東
Lane	小路、車道	Language	語言
Laundromat	洗衣店	Laundry	洗衣店
Law	法律	Leak	漏（氣、水等）
Leaking	漏的	Learn	學
Lease	契約、租	Leave	離開
Left	左，已經離開、左邊	Legal	合法
License	執照、牌照	Light	清淡的
Liquor	烈酒	Little	小的，不多
Location	地點	Long way	遠路
Look forward	盼望	Lot	很多
Low-income area	低收入區	Lumber	木材
Lunch	午餐	Luncheon	（較正式的）午餐
Lyonnais	蛋黃醬	Macaroni	空心通心面
Main dish	主菜	Make	做菜

Market	市場	Master card	萬事達信用卡
Match	火柴	Material	材料
Meal	餐	Mean	意思、意指
Meat	肉	Meatball	肉丸
Menu	菜單	Mess	弄
Metal	金屬	Meter	（水電等）表
Mexican	墨西哥的	Middle	中間
Mild	一點點辣的	Mile	裏，英裏
Mince	剁碎（肉等）	Minced	剁碎的
Minimum	最低限度	Minus	減
Mirror	玻璃鏡	Mistake	過失
Mix	混合，雜的	Mixture	混合物
Money order	匯票	Monthly statement	月結單
More	多，額外的，更多	Motel	汽車旅館
Motor	馬達	Mozzarella Stick	白乳酪條
Must	必定	Near	附近
Need	需要	Next to	隔壁
No	不、沒有	Noisy	吵
Non - smoking area	禁煙區	North (N)	北
Not	不要	Not working	壞了
Notice	示告	Number	號碼
Off	降價、休息	Office	辦公室、寫字樓
Often	經常	On	在
On the side	在側邊	Once	一次
Open	開門、開戶	Opposite	對面、在……對面
Order	訂菜、訂貨	Out of order	壞了

IX. 餐館常用詞 Useful Words

Over	超過	Over - done	太熟
Overcharge	多算	Oyster	蚝油
Pan	平底鍋	Pan - fry	（放平底鍋）煎
Panel	板	Park	停泊車輛、公園
Parking	停車	Parking lot	停車場
Parkway	大公路	Partner	拍檔，合股人
Partnership	合股經營	Pass	經過
Pasta	意大利面條	Pasta sauce	面條調味料
Peel	皮、去皮	Permit	許可證、牌照
Person	人	Personal checking account	私人支票户
Phoenix	鳳	Pickle	腌的
Piece	片、個（pieces復數）	Pilot	火種
Pipe	管道	Pizza (slice)	意大利餅（薄餅）
Place	地點、街	Plain	净的，不加東西的
Platform	臺、架子	Platter	大拼盤
Plaza	有商店的廣場	Plumber	水管工人
Plus	加	Population	人口
Post	張貼	Post office	郵電局
Pour	倒、灌	Power	停電
Practice	練習	Prepare	做菜，制作
Press	按、壓	Price	價格
Private house	私家房	Product	產品
Prosperous	繁榮、景氣	Pt. (pint)	品脱（16安士）
Pudding	布丁（甜點）	Put	放
Qt. (quart)	誇脱（32安士）	Race	種族
Rare	半熟的	Raw	生的

English	Chinese	English	Chinese
Real hot	非常辣	Really	真的
Receipt	收據	Receive	收到
Recommend	推薦	Refund	退錢
Regular hot	一般辣的		
Regular menu	一般菜單（除特別午餐、晚餐、和菜之外的菜）		
Reheat	再熱	Rent	租、租金
Repair	修理	Replace	代替
Report	報告	Reservation	預約（名詞）
Reserve	預訂（動詞）	Residential zone	住宅區
Restaurant	餐館	Return	退回
Right	右	Ring	按鈴
Rinse	衝洗，漂	Roach	蟑螂
Road (Rd)	路	Roast	烘、烤（肉）
Roof	屋頂	Roof tile	瓦
Room	房間	Rotten	腐壞的
Rouse	老鼠	Rule	條例
Rusty	生銹的	Small (S)	小的（份量）
Salad	色拉	Salty	咸的
Sanitary	衛生的	Sanitize	消毒
Sausage	香腸	Sauté	炒（菜）
Saving account	儲蓄户口	School	學校
Scoop	勺	Scramble	炒（指炒蛋）
Screen door	紗窗	Seal	封口
Season	季節	Seat	坐、座位
Send back	送回（原公司）	Separate	分開
Serve	服務，上菜	Service	服務

187

IX. 餐館常用詞 Useful Words

Sesame	芝麻	Set course	套餐（有固定搭配）
Sewer	下水道	Shaker	（裝調味料）瓶
Share	分享	Sharp	鋒利的
Shelf	架子	Shell	殼、去殼
Shell fish	貝殼類	Shopping center	購物中心
Shopping mall	室內的購物中心	Show	帶領、指示
Shred	切絲的	Shredded	切絲的
Sick	病	Side	旁邊
Sign	招牌，簽名（名詞）	Signature	簽名
Simmer	慢煮、煲	Sink	水槽
Sizzling	油炸米放進湯時聲音	Skin	皮、去皮
Slice	切片	Sliced	切片的
Slippery	滑的	Slow	指示（方向）
Smoking area	吸煙區	So on	等等
Soak	浸、泡	Soap	肥皂（粉）
Soft	柔軟的	Soft drink	軟飲料（汽水果汁之類）
Sole proprietorship	單獨經營	Sometimes	有時
Soup	湯	Sour	酸的
Sour cream	酸奶油	South (S)	南
Spaghetti	意大利長麵條	Special	特別（菜）
Spicy	香辣的 (等於hot)	Spill	濺出、流出
Spoil	變壞	Spot	斑點
Sprinkle	灑、撒	Square	廣場
Square foot	平方尺	Stain	污點
Stale	不鮮的	Start with	從……開始
State	州	Stay	停留、保持

English	Chinese	English	Chinese
Steam	煮，蒸	Steamed	蒸的
Stew	炖	Sticky	粘黏的
Stink	臭的	Stir - fry	炒（菜等）
Stoppage	塞住	Storage	薦放（貨物）
Store	商店	Stove	爐竈
Straight	直的、挺直	Strainer	過濾網（器）
Strange	怪的	Street (St)	街
Strong	濃的	Studio	工作室，攝影室
Style	式，種類	Sublease	轉租
Subway - Station	地鐵站	Such as	例如……等等
Suite	房間、套房	Super market	超級市場
Sweet	甜的	Swell	脹
Swollen	膨脹的	System	系統
T.V.	電視	Tag	標簽
Take	點菜	Take out	外賣
Taste	味道	Tasty	好吃的
Tax	稅	Temperature	溫度
Tender	嫩的、柔軟的	Teriyaki	烤（牛肉串等，日本話）
Term	期限、租期	Thaw	解凍
There	那裏	Thermometer	溫度計
Thick	稠的、厚的	Thin	稀的、薄的
Think	想，認爲	Through	穿過
Throw away	扔掉	Time	時間
Tip	小費	To	到
Toast	吐司（面包片）	Too much	太多
Top	上端、加在……頂上	Total	總額

IX. 餐館常用詞 Useful Words

Tough	（肉等）老的、堅韌的	Town	鎮
Toxic	有毒的、中毒	Traffic light	交通燈
Travel	旅游	Traveler	旅行者
Triple	三倍的	Trouble	麻煩
Tunnel	地下道、海底隧道	Turn	轉、轉灣
Turning	轉彎處	Turnpike	收費公路
Twice	兩次	Under - cooked (done)	不夠熟
Unfair	不公平	University	大學
Until (till)	直到	Up	上
Uptown	上城	Utensil	器具
Vacancy	空的	Vacant	空位的
Veneer	貼板	Vent	氣孔
Ventilation system	氣系統	Village	村莊
Vinegary	酸的	Violation	違反
Visa card	維薩信用卡	W. (with)	配、跟有……
Wait for	等待	Waiter	男企臺、男服務生
Waitress	女企臺、女服務生	Walk	走路
Wall paper	墙紙	Wallboard	墙板（水泥板）
Warm	温暖的	Warning	警告
Wash	洗	Watch	看
Water pipe	水管	Way	路、方向、方法
Weak	淡的	Wealthy area	富有地區
Welcome to	歡迎到…	Well done	燒（煮）得熟一點
West (W)	西	Wet	濕的
Wine	酒	Wine list	酒單、酒牌
Wipe	擦	Wish	希望

With	用，與……一起	Withdraw	取錢
Without	不用，沒有	Wood	木
Wooden post (stud)	木條、柱	Writing	寫
Yogurt	酸奶	Zip - code	郵政號碼

餐具與其它設備 Tableware and Accessories

Aluminum plate	鋁盤（銀盤）	Apron	圍裙
Ashtray	烟灰缸	Bag	袋
Booster seat	小孩凳子	Bottle	瓶子
Bowl	碗	Box	盒子
Calculator	計算器	Can	罐頭、鐵罐
Cash register	收錢機	Chair	椅子
Chopstick	筷子	Container	裝食物容器
Counter	櫃臺	Cover	蓋子
Cup	杯子	Foam box	泡沫盒
Foil	金屬紙	Fork	餐叉
Garbage bag	垃圾袋	Glass	玻璃杯，玻璃
Hat	帽	High chair	高椅子
Knife	小刀	Lady's room	女衛生間
Lid	蓋子	Men's room	男衛生間
Napkin	餐巾	Pants	長褲
Paper bag	紙袋	Pen	筆
Pencil	鉛筆	Pint	16號紙盒（16安士）
Pitcher	水壺	Plastic bag	塑料袋
Plate	盤子、碟子	Quart	32號紙盒（32安士）
Rectangular	長方形的	Refrigerator	冰箱

IX. 餐館常用詞 Useful Words

Restroom	衛生間	Round	圓的
Shirt	襯衫	Sign	招牌
Silverware	餐具	Spoon	湯匙
Straw	汽水吸管	Table	桌子
Teapot	茶壺	Teaspoon	茶匙
Telephone	電話	Tissue	紙巾
Toothpick	牙籤	Top	蓋子，上面
Towel	紙巾		

蔬菜類 Vegetables

Almond	杏仁	Asparagus	蘆荀
Baby corn	小玉米	Baby rape	油菜苗
Bamboo shoot	筍片	Bean curd	豆腐
Bean sprout	芽菜	Bitter melon	涼瓜
Bok Choy	白菜（廣東音）	Broccoli	芥蘭
Cabbage	包菜（卷心菜）	Carrot	紅蘿卜
Cashew nut	腰果	Cauliflower	中國花菜
Celery	芹菜		
Chinese cabbage (Napa)		紹菜（黃白菜）	
Chinese vegetable		白菜、小白菜、菜心、	
Cucumber	黃瓜	Curry	咖喱
Dry mushroom	香菇	Eggplant	茄子
Five spicy powder	五香粉	French fries	薯條
Fried bean curd	炸豆腐	Fungus	木耳
Garlic	蒜頭	Garlic shoot	大蒜
Ginger	生姜	Herb	香菜、草藥

Leaf mustard	芥菜	Leek	韭菜
Leek sprout	韭菜花	Lemon	檸檬
Lettuce	生菜、萵苣	Lily flower	金針菜
Liquorices (licorice) root	甘草	Mushroom	蘑菇
Mustard green	芥菜	Onion	洋蔥
Parsley	荷蘭芹	Pea pod	雪豆
Peanut	花生	Pepper	辣椒
Pickled vegetable	酸菜	Potato	馬鈴薯
Preserved sour cabbage	酸菜		
(Star) aniseed	（星形）八角 (茴香的果)		
Scallion	青蔥	Seaweed	紫菜（海菜）
Seaweed or kelp	海帶	Sesame	芝麻
Snow pea	雪豆	Snow peas seedling	豆苗
Snow peas tips (shoot, leaf)	豆苗	Spinach	菠菜
Straw mushroom	草菇	String bean	四季豆
Sweet pea	甜豆（與雪豆相似）		
Tomato	西紅柿	Vegetable	蔬菜（總稱）
Walnut	胡桃	Water chestnut	馬蹄片
Water spinach	通菜（空心菜）	Watercress	西洋菜
White carrots (radish)	白羅卜	Winter melon	冬瓜

米、面、粉類 Rice and Noodles

Almond cookies	杏仁餅	Brown rice	黑飯（已加調味料）
Congee (rice porridge)	粥	Cornstarch	澱粉（生粉）
Dough	生面團（做水餃用的）	Dumpling	水餃
Eye noodle	廣東伊面	Flour	面粉

IX. 餐館常用詞 Useful Words

Fortune cookies	簽語餅	Green bean	綠豆
Ho fun	河粉	Instant noodle	快食面
Mea fun	米粉	Noodle	面條
Preserved bean curd	腐乳	Rice	米
Rice yeast	釀酒米麴	Scallion pancake	蔥油餅
Shrimp chip	蝦片（用米粉炸成的）	Soy bean	黃豆
Soy bean custard	豆漿	Soy bean milk	豆奶
Steamed bun (bread)	饅頭	Sticky rice	八寶糯米飯
Tapioca	西米	Taro	芋頭
Vermicelli (transparent noodle)	粉絲		
White rice	白飯	Wonton	餛飩
Yam (sweet potato)	甘薯	Yeast	酵母

海鮮類 Seafood

Abalone	鮑魚	Bass	鱸魚
Black clam	黑蜆（沙蜆）	Black fish	花斑魚
Carp ship	鯇魚（鯉魚）	Catfish	貓魚（繪魚）
Clam	蛤，蜆	Cod	鱈魚
Conch	海螺（響螺）	Crab	蟹
Crab leg	（長腿）蟹腳	Crucial	（歐州）鯽魚
Cuttlefish	墨魚（烏賊）	Dungeness (green) crab	溫哥華大蟹
Eel	鰻魚	Filet	無骨魚片
Fish	魚	Fish ball	魚丸
Fish maw	魚肚	Fish stick	魚串
Flounder (sole)	龍利（即蝶魚）	Geo-duck clam	象頭蚌（女神蛤）
Jelly fish	海哲皮	Live shrimp	游水蝦

Lobster	龍蝦	Mussel	黑蜆（西方）
Oyster	生蚝	Pollock	青（綠）魚
Prawn	大蝦（明蝦）	Razor (long) clam	刀蜆（竹蜆）
Salmon	鮭魚	Scallop	幹貝
Sea bass	司貝（一種鱸魚）	Sea cucumber	海參
Shark	鯊魚	Shark fern	（鯊）魚翅
Shrimp	蝦	Snail	石螺（田螺）
Snapper	鯛魚		
Snow crab cluster	（長腿）蟹脚		（常帶有胸肉）
Squid	魷魚	Stone fish	石頭魚
Tilapia fish	（非洲）鯽魚	Tuna	金槍魚
Whiting fish	懷寧（一種鯉魚）		

肉類 Meat

Meat	肉（總稱）	Bacon	熏肉片
Beef	牛肉	Beef trip	牛百葉
Beef (cattle) viscera	牛雜	Bird's nest	燕窩（譽巢）
Chicken	雞肉	Chicken wing	雞翅膀
Chicken leg	雞腿	Duck	鴨
Duck feet (hand)	鴨掌（仙掌）	Duck wings	鴨翅膀
Egg	雞蛋	Egg white	蛋白
Filet steak	牛柳	Frog	田雞
Gizzard	腎	Ham	火腿
Intestine	腸	Kidney	腎
Lamb	羊肉：小羊	Liver	肝
Mutton	羊肉	Pig (hog)'s belly (stomach)	豬肚

IX. 餐館常用詞 Useful Words

Pig's hand (knuckle)	豬手	Pork	豬肉
Pork chop	豬排	Poultry	家禽
Rabbit	兔：兔肉	Roast pork	叉燒肉
Spare rib	排骨	Spare rib tip	排骨尾
Squab	乳鴿	Steak	牛排（或牛肉）
Turkey	火雞	Veal	（小牛之）肉
Yolk	蛋黃		

調味料 Sauces

Broth	清湯	Brown sauce	黑碩司（醬汁）
Chili sauce	辣油	Clear soup	清湯
Dressing	調味料	Duck sauce	酸梅醬
Garlic	蒜頭（粉）	Gravy sauce	芙蓉碩司
Hoi sing sauce	海鮮醬 (木須用)	Honey	蜜
Hot oil	辣油	Hot sauce	辣醬
Ingredient	原料	Ketchup	蕃茄醬
M.S.G	味精	Mustard sauce	芥茉醬
Oil	油	Peanut butter	花生醬
Pepper	辣椒（粉）	Sacra	沙茶醬
Salt	鹽	Sauce	醬汁（碩司）
Seasoning	調味料	Soy sauce	醬油
Sugar	糖	Tartar sauce	他他醬（用來醮蝦、魚）
Tomato sauce	蕃茄醬	Vinegar	醋
White sauce	白碩司（醬汁）	Wine	酒

飲料 Beverage

7 up	七喜	Beer	啤酒
Beverage	飲料總稱	Coffee	咖啡
Coke (Coca-Cola)	可樂	Cream soda	奶油汽水
DR. Pepper	辣椒博士	Drink	飲料
Fruit punch	混合果汁	Ginger ale	姜啤
Iced tea	冰茶	Jasmine tea	茉莉茶
Juice	果汁	Lemonade	檸檬水
Milk	牛奶	Mineral water	礦泉水
Pepsi	百事可樂	Root beer	根口啤
Slice	薄片	Soda	汽水
Spring water	礦泉水	Sprite	雪碧

水果 Fruits

Apple	蘋果	Banana	香蕉	Cherry 櫻桃	Coconut 椰子果
Date	棗			Grape	葡萄
Green banana	未熟的香蕉			Honeydew	哈密瓜
Leeched	荔枝			Lemon	檸檬
Long an	龍眼			Loquat	枇杷
Lotus seed	蓮子			Mango	芒果
Orange	橘子			Peach	桃
Pear	梨			Pineapple	菠籮
Plantain	大香蕉（炸着吃，不能生吃；也有 green 與 sweet 之分）				
Plum	酸莓，李子			Strawberry	草莓
Sweet banana	熟的香蕉	Tangerine	橘子	Watermelon	西瓜

X.附錄
Appendix

食物成語 Food Idiom

A piece of Cake	十分容易	Very easy
Bad egg	壞蛋，惡棍	Scoundrel
Be nuts about	…對…十分熱	Crazy about
Big cheese	老板	Boss
Bread and butter	食物	Food
Bring home the bacon	謀生	Make a living
Butter somebody up	奉承某人	Flatter somebody
Chew the fat	閒聊	Chat
Gravy train	輕鬆可掙的大錢	Big money easy way
Half-baked	還不成熟的	Not yet mature
Hot potatoes	燙手山芋，棘手問題	Problematic issues
In a nutshell	根本上說	Basically
Nutty as a fruitcake	有點瘋狂	A little crazy
One smart cookie	聰明人	Intelligent person
One's cup of tea	某人所喜歡的人或物	The type of person or stuff one likes
Out to lunch	有點脫離現實	A little out of touch with reality
Polish the apple	拍馬屁	Flatter
Spilt the beans	吐露秘密	Share confidential information
The cream of the crop	最優秀的人	The best
Use one's noodles	思考	Think

美國50個州州名，簡寫及首府
The States, the State Capitals and The Abbreviations

州名	State	州名簡寫 Abbreviation	首府	State Capital
阿拉巴馬州	Alabama	AL	蒙哥馬利	Montgomery
阿拉斯加州	Alaska	AK	朱諾	Juneau
阿利桑那州	Arizona	AZ	菲尼克斯	Phoenix
阿肯色州	Arkansas	AR	小石城	Little rock
加利福尼亞州	California	CA	薩克拉門托	Sacramento
科羅拉多州	Colorado	CO	丹佛	Denver
康涅狄格州	Connecticut	CT	哈特福德	Hartford
特拉華州	Delaware	DE	多佛	Dover
佛羅裏達州	Florida	FL	塔拉哈西	Tallahassee
喬治亞州	Georgia	GA	亞特蘭大	Atlanta
夏威夷州	Hawaii	HI	檀香山	Honolulu
愛達荷州	Idaho	ID	博伊西	Boise
伊利諾斯州	Illinois	IL	斯普林菲爾德	Springfield
印第安納州	Indiana	IN	印第安納波利斯	Indianapolis
愛荷華州	Iowa	IA	得梅因	Des Moines
堪薩斯州	Kansas	KS	托皮卡	Topeka
肯塔基州	Kentucky	KY	法蘭克福	Frankfort
路易斯安那州	Louisiana	LA	巴吞魯日	Baton Rouge

緬因州	Maine	ME	奧古斯塔	Augusta
馬裏蘭州	Maryland	MD	安納波利斯	Annapolis
馬薩諸塞州	Massachusetts	MA	波士頓	Boston
密歇根州	Michigan	MI	蘭辛	Lansing
明尼蘇達州	Minnesota	MN	聖保羅	St. Paul
密西西比州	Mississippi	MS	杰克遜	Jackson
密蘇裏州	Missouri	MO	杰斐遜城	Jefferson City
蒙大拿州	Montana	MT	海倫娜	Helena
內布拉斯加州	Nebraska	NE	林肯	Lincoln
內華達州	Nevada	NV	卡森城	Carson City
新罕布什爾州	New Hampshire	NH	康科德	Concord
新澤西州	New jersey	NJ	特倫頓	Trenton
新墨西哥州	New Mexico	NM	聖菲	Santa Fe
紐約州	New York	NY	奧爾巴尼	Albany
北卡羅來納州	North Carolina	NC	納羅利	Raleigh
北達科他州	North Dakota	ND	俾斯麥	Bismarck
俄亥俄州	Ohio	OH	哥倫布	Columbus
俄克拉荷馬州	Oklahoma	OK	俄克拉何馬城	Oklahoma City
俄勒岡州	Oregon	OR	塞勒姆	Salem
賓夕法尼亞州	Pennsylvania	PA	哈裏斯堡	Harrisburg
羅得島州	Rhode Island	RL	普羅維登斯	Providence
南卡羅來納州	South Carolina	SC	哥倫比亞	Columbia

X. 附錄　Appendix

南達科他州	South Dakota	SD	皮爾	Pierre
田納西州	Tennessee	TN	納什維爾	Nashville
得克薩斯州	Texas	TX	奧斯汀	Austin
猶他州	Utah	UT	鹽湖城	Salt Lake City
佛蒙特州	Vermont	VT	蒙彼利埃	Montpelier
弗吉尼亞州	Virginia	VA	裏士滿	Richmond
華盛頓州	Washington	WA	奧林匹亞	Olympia
西弗吉尼亞州	West Virginia	WV	查爾斯頓	Charleston
威斯康辛州	Wisconsin	WI	麥迪遜	Madison
懷俄明州	Wyoming	WY	夏延	Cheyenne

幹煸四季豆 Dry-Fried French Beans with Minced Pork

大閘蟹
Crabs

紅棗香雞
JuJube Chicken

刺身拼盤
Shashimi Plate

紅燒雞塊
Roast Chicken Slices

頂級刺身拼盤
Jumbo Shashimi Plate

葱油拌面
Noodles Mixed with Scallion

加拿大象拔蚌
Canada Geoduck

三文治
Sandwich

三文魚北極貝刺身
Salmon & Surf Clam Sashimi

沙爹羊腩煲
Satay Lamp Casserole

加洲卷
Calinfornia Roll

梅幹菜扣肉 Pork with Preserved Vegetable

家常紅燒魚 Family Style Braised Fish with Soy Sauce

涼瓜小炒
Bitter Melon

餃子
Dumplings

手拍青瓜 Cucumber

鷄 Chicken

西湖醋魚 Sweet and Sour West Lake Fish

鐵板黑椒牛排 Hot Plate Beef with Pepper

鐵板茄子 Hot Plate Eggplant

羊肉串燒烤 Barbecue Lamb Shashlik

豬手 Pork Trotters

麻婆豆腐醬 CookDo Mabo Tofu Sauce

205

幹草菇
Dried Shitake Mushrooms

Hontsuyu, Soup Base for Noodle

烹煮米酒 Mirin, Sweet Cooking Rice Wine

醬油
Okonomi Sauce

日式辣 Japanese Mixed Chili Pepper

辣椒油 La-Yu Chili Oil with Chili Pepper

Japanese-style Barbeque sauce 日式燒烤醬

日本薄餅
Japanese Pizza

天婦羅雜會
Tempura Mix, Tempurak

Tamanoi Sushinoko

芥末綠豆
Wasabi Green Pea

烤紫菜
Roasted Seaweed

壽司米
Sushi Rice

麻油
sesame oil

醬油
Ponzu Sauce

醋
Seasoned Rice Vinegar

龜甲萬燒烤醬油 Kikkoman
Teriyaki Marinade & Sauce

海天特級草菇醬油
Premium Mushroom Soy Sauce

萬字醬油 KIKKOMAN
Naturally Brewed Soy Sauce

燒烤醬
YaKiniku BBQ Sauce

上字壽司醬 YAMASA
Sushi Soy Sauce

白醋
White Rice Vinegar

芥末膏 Wasabi, Prepared in Tube

有機醬油 Wheat Free and Organic Soy Sauce